Higher

A BUTCH FOR BUTCH ROMANCE

ROZ ALEXANDER

This is a work of fiction. Names, characters, places, events, and incidents are either the product of the author's imagination or within the public domain. Any resemblance to real people (living or dead), places, or events is entirely coincidental.

Higher

First edition. May 1, 2021.

Copyright © 2021 Roz Alexander.

Written by Roz Alexander

Cover design by Roz Alexander

All rights reserved, including the right to reproduce this book. This book is for your personal enjoyment only.

If you would like to use material from this book (other than for review purposes), prior written permission must be obtained by contacting the author.

Copyright © 2021 Roz Alexander
All rights reserved.
ISBN: 9798201731304

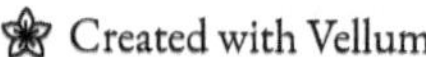 Created with Vellum

For all my butch4butches out there

Blurb

Where do dreams go to wait?

Tali Blue is going back to finish rabbinical school…eventually. When she returned to her hometown seven years ago to help her grandparents raise her younger sisters, she planned on it being temporary. Now she has a stable job and a stable life surrounded by the people she's known forever. It's all just *fine* —and then there's the incredibly annoying surprise of Maple.

Maple never meant to be successful. She just wanted to make weird art and practice her Ladino. And just like that, 15 years of adulthood has built a solid career, a great reputation as an art instructor, and a lackluster love life. It doesn't help that she's strictly a butch-for-butch lesbian. And then comes a sex goddess in the form of short, chunky, smoking hot, and incredibly nervous, butch Tali Blue.

When Tali's love of family, Maple's art ambitions, and a Rosh Hashanah effort to #savethebees force these two together, both of them may learn that the only way out is up, together.

This new year the honey is dripping on a lot more than apples. *Higher* is a steamy, butch-for-butch, grump-sunshine lesbian romance about what happens when you choose to take your dreams higher.

Also by Roz

HOT FOR THE HOLIDAYS SERIES

Matzo Match

Higher

A Masc for Purim

STEAMY FRIDAY NIGHT SHORTS

Light My Candles: A Friends-to-Lovers Romance

Bring Me Home: A Butch-for-Butch Romance

OTHER WORKS

Rooting for You: A Butch-for-Butch Small Town Romance

The Office Party: A Butch-for-Butch Erotic Short

Note from Roz

This story is about two Jewish, butch queer women. This entire series ("Hot for the Holidays") is about queer Jewish people falling in love and having hot, explicit sex. Sex in Judaism is celebrated, is a mitzvah (a good deed/a commandment), is divine. These stories are meant to honor and uplift Jewish love (including interfaith love) and also to be lovingly honest and hopeful about the modern Jewish community.

And, mostly, I wanted to write some gay, Jewish smut.

The Jewish community includes people of a multitude of races, genders, sexualities, and abilities, as well as a wide spectrum of beliefs and practices. There's no one "right" way to be or do Jewish — and the absence of an identity or belief here is not a condemnation on my part.

This story contains: absent parent (father), adoption, angst (lots!), butt stuff, deceased parent (mom), explicit sex, external and internalized homophobia/butchphobia (if you want to skip the explicit external homophobia, skip chapter 16), honey on skin, migraine (on page and historical), penetration, pet names, phone sex, sibling dynamics, and, as always, an HEA (Happily Ever After)

On butch identity: Someone once told me that their definition of "butch" was "anyone who is masculine who the world thinks should not be." I like it for its simplicity, though no definition can hold the complexities and histories of butch identity, pain, joy, and liberation. This story is about two butches falling in love. It's also set in a world, our world, that believes butches can be many different things.

And specifically regarding stone butch identity: I have had the pleasure of knowing quite a few stone butches in my life. It's a term that I think is falling out of popularity in favor of some other, newer terms, but for these folks, it's the one that still feels like it fits. There are many, many different ways of being a stone butch, not just what is depicted in this story, and I am grateful to all my pals and sensitivity readers who've shared their thoughts and edits with me.

If any of that doesn't fit what you want/need from a story right now—this might not be the one for you.

B'Simcha (in joy) and happy new year,
Roz

Glossary

Note: because many of these words are translated and/or transliterated, there are multiple accepted spellings. These are also the simplest definitions, and if you're interested, I encourage you to dig deeper into each!

Ashkenazi – Jews who are from, directly or indirectly, Eastern European countries

Bubbe – Yiddish for grandmother

Days of Awe – the High Holy Days: Rosh Hashanah, Yom Kippur, and the days in-between

D'var/dvar – a short way of saying "d'var torah"; literally "a word" refers to a short speech about a Torah passage.

Hebrew – Semitic language spoken by multiple Jewish communities

High Holidays – the Jewish holy days of Rosh Hashanah and Yom Kippur

Kippah – the Hebrew word for the small, round, cloth head covering ("brimless hat") some Jews wear; called a yarmulke in Yiddish

Ladino – Romance language spoken by some Sephardic Jews

Rosh Hashanah – the Jewish New Year, often a two-day long festival, begins the ten days of penitence and reflection that culminates with Yom Kippur.

Sephardic – Jews who are descended from the Jewish populations that left Spain and Portugal in the late 15th century

Shabbat – the best holiday (okay, that's just my opinion), but it *is* the holiest holiday, and it's every week. Shabbat is (in simplest terms) from sundown on Friday to sundown on Saturday, a day of rest when work is forbidden. (Jews observe, or don't observe, this in many different ways.)

Shabbat Candles – the blessing that welcomes in Shabbat each week is the lighting of the candles. (Some households do two per person, some two per household, some light even more just in case there are people out there unable to light for themselves.)

Synagogue/Temple – the building for Jewish congregations

Tikkun Olam – literally "world repair," this is one of the things the Jewish people have been tasked with: repairing the world.

Yiddish – Germanic language spoken by some Ashkenazi Jews

Yom Kippur – the Day of Atonement, many Jews fast on this day and wear white.

Zayde – Yiddish for grandfather

Spring

Texts sent between two of the Blue sisters when one was definitely too hangry to receive it.

Anna: Did you know that native bees are like 3 times better at pollinating than honey bees? THREE TIMES.

Tali: Anna, I swear, if you bring this up one more time, I'm going to lose it. You. Are. Not. Working. For. Me.

Anna: AND

Tali: uuuuugggghhhh

Anna: I mean, our other pollination options are like wasps and MOSQUITOS—doesn't that make you want to #SaveTheBees????

One — Tali

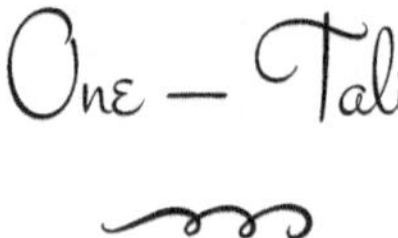

Tali felt her cheek muscles tense into a grimace and worried about a migraine coming on.

"Pleeeeease!" Anna stretched out the vowels so the word became more sound than meaning.

Tali would give her sister ten more seconds of mono-loguing time. Then she would throw her from the office. Not physically. Anna might be the youngest, but she was almost a full foot taller than Tali.

Beth, the middle sister, was also taller than Tali, but just by an inch or two. And, if she was being honest, she knew that at 5'1", it was a low bar.

"If your plan is to wear me down—"

"Is it working?" The hope in that short question was over-whelming. Anna had been trying to persuade her all morning. And all week. And since last Fall.

"No. I told you I don't want to discuss this. You getting a job here is a slippery slope."

"You mean it's your slippery slope." *Ouch.*

"Anna—"

"No, sorry. That was unfair. I take it back. I take it back! It's just...well, Tal, you and I are really different people!"

"Duh." Something about sisters, even ones that you sort of raised, brought out the childish side.

"And you said last, like, October that I could apply for this program!"

"What I remember saying was that you could apply as long as you *also* applied to some state schools." Tali tried to sound stern, which wasn't as hard as she wished it was. *Every year I'm becoming a bit more like our grandmother. A hard, unbending woman. But Bubbe also loves a whole lot. I should learn some of that. Ugh, what if I'm already an old woman at 33?* "I never actually said yes to a gap year at all."

"I applied!" Her voice a whisper-shout so she wouldn't be heard through the thin walls of the synagogue offices. "I applied to the state schools. I don't find out until the end of this month."

"Okay, well, let's see how that goes, and then—"

"Tali." Her kid sister's face was carefully arranged in a take-no-shit mask that Tali didn't buy for a second. If there was anything Tali knew for sure about her sister, it was that she was as moveable and flighty as a dandelion. "I don't need your consent. I'm about to be an adult. I get to choose my own life, and this is what I want!"

Tali grunted. Her opponent was perched on the edge of one of the wooden chairs that faced Tali's desk. Her spine was rod straight while Tali seemed to be slouching further into her own office chair with each passing moment.

Sometimes she wondered how Anna had turned out so different from her. She loved the ballet lessons that Tali had been paying for the last seven years, and she loved to wear flowy, pastel dresses and oversized sweaters. Tali only worked out when it occurred to her she should a couple of times a month. Her entire wardrobe was button-ups and slacks, except for the occasional sweater, which she put over a button-up. She supposed Beth fell somewhere in-between the two of them on this as well.

A spectrum, the Blue sisters.

"Now, if you're going to be supportive, what I need is to help with planning a big program here. Will you hire me or not?"

Anna crossed her bare arms over her daisy print sky blue dress and leaned back in her chair with the easy confidence of the youngest child who's never heard 'no.'

She is getting on my every last nerve. Tali searched her face, so similar to what she still saw of their mother's when she closed her eyes, and something there caught her off guard. Never before had she seen that look of determination on her sister's features.

On the rare occasions she told Anna no, the teen would give up, usually because she'd already come up with a whole new idea by then. This, she realized, had been totally different. For months Anna had been talking about a super-selective program in Berlin their other sister had sent her a brochure for.

"I don't like it," Tali admitted, though Anna's expression in response showed how clear that already was. "You have to still consider the other schools."

"Fine, sure." Anna realized she'd finally made headway, and she leaned closer to the desk. "So, you'll help me with this?"

Tali let out a long sigh but couldn't help but let her lips curve into the tiniest smile.

"Yes, let me pull up my calendar," Tali turned back to her laptop and found the Fall schedule for the temple. "Every holiday is super planned out until like Rosh Hashanah in September. Isn't that too close to the application deadline?"

"No! That's perfect. It doesn't have to be a completed

program, just a real, planned one. And they have a whole process for sending them updates during the application review," Anna was practically vibrating with excitement. Tali expected she'd float across the room if she got any happier. "Oh! Tali, you're the BEST."

"Stop yelling. You'll get me fired," Tali grumbled back at her as she typed notes into the synagogue's shared calendar about the Rosh Hashanah plan. "And you'll have to have already accepted another school offer by then. I don't like this. But, ugh, fine. It'll have to be Rosh Hashanah day. Maybe a lunchtime program between services. What's your next step, kid?"

"Okay, first of all, rabbi Simon will *never* fire you. You do too much around here," Anna said, ignoring Tali's eye roll. "And there's this artist who's been doing really cool stuff with nature and Jewish stuff, and she only lives like 45 minutes upstate. Buuuuut she's going to this bee garden next week that's like six hours away, and I was hoping you could go for me."

The puppy dog eyes were back, and Tali's defenses were already down, so she said yes.

"But I have to talk to Simon first."

After Anna left, Tali made the journey down the hall to rabbi Simon's office. She found him like she always did: leaning too close to the computer screen, squinting, one hand on his kippah as if it would shoot off in surprise when he deciphered whatever code he was scrutinizing.

"When will you admit you need glasses?"

"When will you learn to respect your elders?" He shot

back without moving from his position.

"Simon, you're five years older than me. How much more respect should I expect to gain in my next five years?" She settled into the chair that she thought of as her chair. It wasn't. It was the chair of anxious parents promising they'd be a valuable member of the synagogue if only he'd help get their kid ready for the impending b'mitzvah that they definitely had not planned appropriately for. It was the chair of half of a hopeful couple staring dewy-eyed at their partner in the identical chair next to it while they talked about their wedding ceremony and which rituals felt right to them. It was the chair of grieving widows seeking counsel and bored kids trying to get out of Hebrew tutoring.

But it was also the chair she'd found herself in almost every day for the last seven years since she'd started here as his assistant.

"Well, I finished rabbinical school, so think about what kind of respect you'd get if you decided to do the same."

"Low blow, man, low blow." But she laughed anyway. The sting of her last semester dropout status had mostly worn off years prior, tied up in the same grieving process that had led to her leaving school in the first place. "Also, you know you can make the text bigger on the screen, right?"

"As you pointed out, I'm barely older than you. Technically a millennial, I think. I know how to use a computer. It's not my problem you don't like the way I sit."

Tali rolled her eyes, but since he was glued to his screen, she didn't have to worry about him seeing it.

"What are you looking at? We need to head out. The venue walkthrough for Passover's in like fifteen minutes."

"Yeah, yeah, I figured you'd come collect me when it was time," he said with enough gratitude that Tali perked up a little.

It's nice to be needed. I'm still needed here. Not everyone needs to be a rabbi.

"And what I'm looking at is a small scandal."

"A scandal?" Tali snorted. "A temple scandal?"

"You laugh now, but that's because you're not the target of this aggression."

"Aggression! Simon, what are you talking about?"

"On the temple forum. Unbelievable. Some anonymous user has posted a scathing review of my sermons."

"What?" Tali straightened up at that. She knew how deeply Simon cared about his congregation and how much work he put into his weekly sermons. "What does it say?"

"Listen to this," he said, leaning even closer to the screen and pointing at it with the hand not holding his head. Then he read the comment to her, his voice rising to higher and higher pitches with each sentence. "R'Simon is a nice man, and his speeches are usually pretty spot on. The snacks he provides though (the cookies) are actually disgusting. No one wants to chip a tooth on a hockey puck masquerading as a dessert. Aren't rabbis supposed to care for the whole person? Not just the Jewish part?"

When he was finished, he swiveled in his chair to stare into her eyes, his brow furrowed in dismay. "Can you *believe* that?"

Tali tried her best, she did, but after a moment of trying to look serious and contemplative, she burst out laughing.

"Oh, this is all a joke to you?" His voice continued to be shrill, which only made her laugh harder until she was clutching the arms of her chair and wheezing. She took a few deep breaths to calm down before finding the strength to respond to him.

"Simon, the cookies you get *are* terrible. You buy them from that dusty old bakery down the street every single time, even though no one ever eats them. Honestly, I thought we must get them for free or something. I couldn't understand why you kept doing it."

"I like those cookies!" Simon looked outraged, and Tali decided to make eye contact with the painting over his shoulder so that she could keep a straight face. "I've been eating them since I was a kid, and my grandpa would walk me there before services. Mrs. McCutcheon is a very nice woman and a master baker!"

"Well, it seems that you're at a crossroads here, boss. Win hearts and minds with words alone, or go for the age-old strategy of winning the people over through their stomachs."

Simon made a sound like an old dog being forced to learn to play dead before letting out a long breath and turning a calmer expression in her direction.

"Fine, I'll think about it. Maybe I'll make you buy the cookies next time."

"Happy to."

"What did you come in here to talk about? Just to collect me for the meeting?"

"Oh, we can move onto less serious agenda items now that we've discussed the great dessert catastrophe?"

"Don't tease me. I'm feeling fragile," he said while clutching his chest in mock agony.

"Fine, fine. I came in to talk about High Holidays. Rosh Hashanah specifically, I think."

"Wow, getting an early start this year. Don't we have a meeting set to discuss this in two or three months?" He started packing up his desk into the ancient, worn brown backpack he used to travel between locations. Her heart gave a little squeeze, and she realized again how lucky she felt to work for this human and consider him a friend.

"Yes, we do. Anna came by this morning, though," she said. "And she's trying to get into some German program instead of college."

"Trying to get out of college? That doesn't sound like a

Blue sister move at all," Simon said, his voice drenched in sarcasm.

"Shut it, you. She's already applied to backup schools, but she's dead set on this program. I don't know how likely it is, but in order to apply, she needs to showcase an innovative program she's designed."

"I mean, it sounds cool."

"Sure, yeah, and I'll admit in the secret circle of this office that I'm proud of how hard she's pushing."

"Is it inspiring you to give it another go?" His tone was light, as if this was a casual question and not part of his weekly attempt to get her re-enrolled.

"So, anyway," she said, ignoring him. "She's trying to convince me to let her design the lobby for Rosh Hashanah and a Save the Bees campaign to go along with it."

"Bees?"

"You know, apples and honey for Rosh, so, yeah, bees."

"Got it." He stood up, all of his items carefully stored in their respective pockets, and she joined him as they headed into the hall.

"I told her I'd have to talk to you about it before I head up to meet this artist she wants us to work with."

"You have the budget for the programs for this year. Why do you need me?"

"Well, I thought if you said no then I could make you the bad guy—"

"Okay, so, I think you already know I'm not going to say no," Simon laughed as he locked his office and led them toward the parking lot. "Man, it must be hard to argue with a younger, more energetic version of yourself, huh?"

"Tell me about it." If she thought about it, she knew this was the right move. She *wanted* Anna to have everything she wanted out of life, even if Germany was far away. Really far away.

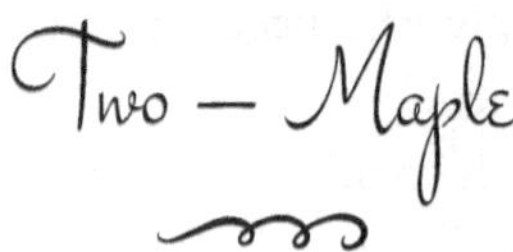

"Maple! How the hell are ya?" Mike managed enough enthusiasm that Maple believed he was happy to see her. But then again, he was a middle-aged bartender in a sleepy town, and tips were a significant part of his livelihood, so that could be it too. She chose to believe he was delighted to see her, though.

"Alive as ever," she shot back, a broad smile stretching her cheeks. She loved being in this town. She kept catching herself prematurely missing it, now that she knew she'd only be back a few more times. "Give me the usual, bud."

Her usual was juice, whatever juice was closest at hand, and she always paid beer price for it. Some bartenders liked to give her shit for it, but she'd become immune to their judgment over the years. Alcohol just didn't do it for her, but nothing beat the atmosphere of a bar for clearing her head.

"Sure thing. What're you doing back, though? I thought you said—"

"Yeah, yeah. I know I talked a big game with the goodbyes, but I needed some more inspiration."

He nodded and made a show of adding two different

juices into a shaker with ice, pouring it into a high ball glass, and garnishing with an orange slice. She felt her eyes go wide, not so secretly pleased at his commitment to her request.

"And the weirdest thing. Got an email from some high school kid hiring me for her temple's High Holiday stuff. Some stuffy rabbi wants to come see the bees with me, talk shop."

"Is that a normal Jew thing? Bee visits?" He asked as he set the glass in front of her.

"Don't think so, but I don't have much experience with rabbis. I told the kid to have him meet me at the apiary in the morning." She took a sip of her juice and exaggerated the look of pleasure. "You've outdone yourself this time, Mike."

"Ah, shove it, ya weird bee pervert."

Maple laughed and pulled out her notepad as he walked away to pour another round of beers for the group of old white men at the other side of the room. Most other artists she knew sketched when something caught their eye, but she'd always written herself notes and turned them into images later. But it'd been a while. She was stuck. Though the inspiration felt like a fire hydrant wrenched open in summer, her ability to translate it into art had come to a screeching halt.

She'd hoped the bees would help.

Sometime after Mike had poured her a tall glass of water, the bar door swung open, and Maple gaped at the entryway. A short, white, chunky, *hot* butch in a baseball cap stood in the doorway, looking intensely uncomfortable. And maybe a little pissed off?

Well, talk about an abundance of inspiration! Maybe this is what she needed, a good roll in the hay to make her brain shut up, lose control, and let the art through.

And sex could surely be art.

She was imagining what excuse she'd use to walk over and talk up this stranger, when the stranger walked straight up to her. She pretended she'd been looking at the mounted screen on the wall over their shoulder, which, *ew*, was broadcasting a golf game.

"Excuse me, is someone sitting here?" The newcomer indicated the stool next to Maple. Weirdly not in the way she'd hoped, not in a *this seat taken?* kind of way.

I mean, this butch isn't even looking at me. How annoying that intentions couldn't be communicated through pheromones or something.

Then again, they were trying to sit right next to her when almost the whole bar was empty. Oh no. What if she had sold the golf watching too well, and they wanted to come talk about this stupid sport with her? *Just answer them, you ninny.*

"Uh, no, not at all." *Great, good job, team. Halfway to falling in love already, for sure.*

"Thanks," they said, still not making eye contact. Instead, they looked around the room, resting their forearms on the edge of the bar, wincing when their eye caught the sports game. *Yes! They hate golf too! Or golf has seriously wronged them in some irreparable way. Either way, this is my in as a fellow golf hater.*

"Who's your friend?" Mike asked as he walked up, interrupting Maple's constant stream of internal overthinking.

"We don't know each other," the stranger said almost before Mike had finished asking.

And the speed of the answer was good because Maple seemed to be possessed by some sort of reckless flirtatious energy since their arrival, and she had almost said *my fate* for no good reason. Best case scenario, this butch would laugh, and they'd flirt and fall in love forever.

More likely scenario: a scathing look and request for a whole lot more space would be in her future. *What is up with me?* It hadn't been *that* long since her last fling. Still, she had been so absorbed with work, or rather, her inability to produce work, that romance and sex had been a definite afterthought for ... a while.

The speed of the answer could also be worrisome. Did it mean that they didn't *want* to know her? That, in fact, this stranger was only interested in men and didn't want anyone to get any ideas about two butches sitting together? Or like, was homophobic, clearly gay or not, and thought two butches together was gross?

Maple. Get. A. Grip. It was just a factual statement!

"I'll take whatever stout you have," the stranger said, making eye contact with something inanimate on the wall. Mike made a funny little face at "stout" before heading into the back, presumably to find out if they had a stout.

"What even is a stout?" Maple asked and then kicked herself. *I don't want to talk about beer! Go back to the golf idea. You know just as much about that.*

"Honestly, no idea," the newcomer admitted, making shy eye contact with her. "I don't like beer, but I panicked. So, now I'm drinking a stout when he finds one, I guess."

Maple laughed and took advantage of the laughter to give this queer another once over. A button-up, nice jeans, a ball cap for some sports team she'd never heard of, and a shoulder bag with a few pins, including one that had "she/her" on it.

"Those your pronouns?" She asked, pointing at the pin.

"Those are the ones. You?"

"Same," Maple said and looked over her shoulder to see if Mike was ever returning, but still no sign of him.

"You a fruity drink fan?" She asked, and then her pale skin went scarlet. "I meant, like cocktails that are fruit-forward. I wasn't using fruity to mean, uh—"

"Gay," Maple said, laughing. This was going way better than expected. She wasn't the one shoving her own foot down her throat for once. "It's just juice. I don't drink. And I am. Gay."

"Oh," the butch said, making uncertain eye contact. *Her eyes are so gray and so round.* "Yeah, same."

"You don't drink either?" Maple asked, teasing. "What're you going to do with that stout then? Pour it in your butch bag?"

"No, what?" She seemed irritated, and for some reason, that made Maple want to annoy her more. *What am I? A 12-year-old boy? Man, you are out of practice.* "I meant I'm gay. Also."

"Yeah, I could tell."

"What, you have some NASA-tuned gaydar?" The stranger looked around the bar, maybe to worry about who had heard all the homosexual talk. Maybe to see if Mike was on his way back, bottle in hand, or if she could be relieved of having to sip whatever a stout ended up being.

"Honey, people on the moon can tell you're gay, with or without NASA's help. You've got butch swagger for *days*."

That heated the shorter woman's face again, and Maple couldn't tell if it was in a good way or not until the response came.

"Mmm, maybe that's true. Or maybe I'm a straight, hard-working Midwestern woman with no time for makeup." Those eyes were now searing into her own, and Maple felt a challenge in them. "How do you know it's not that?"

"Because I'm not attracted to straight women," Maple shot back, allowing herself to lean a little closer, her arm sliding along the bar top towards the other butch.

"That's a ridiculous thing—Wait. Are you flirting with me?" There was genuine surprise in her voice, her eyes back to looking around the room.

Just look at me. There's no one else in the world but us. There was also a little nerves and a whole lot of want.

"Wow, you're quick," Maple teased and then let her hand do what it had wanted since the seat had been taken—she trailed her fingertips ever so lightly down the other woman's arm. The stranger shivered but didn't pull away.

"I think you're the fast one. We *just* met." Something a little playful, or at least curious, was behind those words.

"Isn't that half the fun of it?" She could feel her mouth pulling into a mischievous smile. Oh, this woman was so attractive. Soft and round in all the ways that made Maple's stomach clench, and sharp steel behind each word and movement.

"You're butch," the stranger said flatly, and Maple laughed without pulling back.

"Yeah, baby, butch for butch. Let me show you how good that can be." Her fingers had kept up their gentle movement, but then her wrist was caught in the other woman's grasp.

"Let's go," was all she said, her voice a starving rasp. Maple threw more cash than could possibly have been needed for her juice and the mystery stout, and she pulled the other woman out into the parking lot.

"I'm staying above this bar," Maple said, her fingers around the willing wrist. "The entrance is in the back."

They made it around the building and to the bottom of the loft stairs before either of them spoke. Maple pulled the door open, holding it and waving the stranger in. However, the other woman stood still, looking into the dark expanse of the hallway without moving.

"Changed your mind?" Maple asked, her voice teasing but her heart dropping a little.

"No." The shorter butch shook her head and then pulled her eyes away from the stairs to make eye contact with Maple.

She stepped forward, her hand pushing against Maple's chest, pinning her to the door. "I need to do this before we go up there."

And then her mouth was on Maple's. Her lips so full, so soft and warm. Maple wondered if this stranger was standing on tiptoe to reach her. She wondered why she thought that was so cute. She wondered why she felt frozen in place, except that maybe she was afraid. *Am I? What if this isn't real?*

But that thought was too confusing for this perfect moment of being trapped between a butch and a hard place. Instead, she kissed her back, over and over and over until she needed them to get up those stairs like an ache.

"Let's go," Maple whispered hoarsely as she pulled back from the kiss. The other woman settled back on her heels, her expression glazed over with desire. *Is that what I look like, too? Ready to burst with need?* "After you."

And this time, the stranger did go into the hall, waiting for a moment as Maple locked the door behind them, letting eyes adjust to even darker darkness before climbing up.

On previous stays, Maple had wished for a light in this hall because she was sure she'd trip on a stair and break something one night. Tonight she cursed the lack of light for taking away the chance to check out this short, hot butch's ass. *Sigh.*

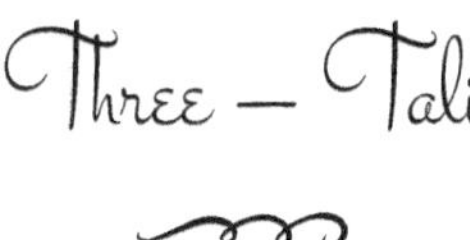

Three — Tali

It had been a while since Tali had been naked in a room with another woman. Sure, her grandmother had set her up on plenty of dates with plenty of nice young women from synagogue families. *Ew, don't think about Bubbe right now.* But most of them were one-date situations. A few makeouts here and there, and also a lot of nothing.

Then there was the butch of it all. How had she never realized how hot other butches were? Was this some sort of internalized homophobia she needed to talk about in therapy? Would her middle-aged, straight-lady therapist understand what she was saying?

Carol does her best. She'll get it. Or pretend to.

The other woman turned from where she was setting down her backpack and emptying her pockets. She was gorgeous. So tall, with warm, brown skin and shining curls wrapped up in a bun above shaved sides. Her eyebrows were full but sharply angled. Tali was overwhelmed by a desire to lick them.

Before the stranger could move or speak again, Tali looped her fingers through the straps of the overalls and yanked her close. Their hips met, pushing against one another as their hands found holds in clothing and on biceps.

Their mouths seemed starved for one another, seeking out frantic patterns. If Tali was even one ounce less horny, she would have worried she was coming across as desperate. But instead, she luxuriated in the feeling that this muscly, tall, richly tan butch seemed to want her just as much. It sent jolts through her body. She ground against the stranger until she moaned.

There was no denying it. This woman in front of her was smoking hot, and she couldn't wait to make her scream her name. Oh, her name.

"Uh, I'm Tali."

When the taller woman pulled back, Tali swore she saw her grimace at the introduction. *Uh oh, is it a Jewish thing?*

"And I'm Jewish." *Well, that'll clear it up.*

"Yeah, I got the Jewish part." She laughed, pointing at the Star of David necklace hanging against Tali's button-up. "I'm also Jewish. But Tali? As in Tali Blue?"

Now it was Tali's turn to pull back. In fact, to take a full step back. "What? How do you know that?"

The painfully attractive queer sighed and ran a palm over her messy bun. "Well, that's a fun, small world."

"What is?" Tali could feel her heart pounding and was suddenly on the verge of panicking. She was in the middle of nowhere. No one should know her name. Except—*Oh, shit.*

"Maple," the artist said, sticking out her hand. "Nice to meet you."

Tali took the other woman's hand in her own, feeling numb. The warm skin against her now icy palm felt new, different from the palm pressed against her ass downstairs. A professional palm.

"Well, this is weird," Tali managed after a pause. "And embarrassing."

"It doesn't need to be either of those things," Maple said, taking back her hand. "We can still have our fun and then make it professional in the morning."

"Uh—"

"I mean," Maple started before taking a step closer to Tali and resting her hands on the shorter woman's hips. "I felt like we were headed in a good direction."

That voice would be the death of Tali. She was certain of it. So deep and smooth. So confident in its crisp enunciation. She wanted to fuck that voice.

No, I'm not fucking anything to do with this person! This, this...colleague!

And yet, there seemed to be currents traveling from Maple's fingers straight through her clothing into Tali's core. She took a deep breath to center herself and get ready to step away, to make the professional decision.

Then she made the mistake of looking up into those warm brown eyes, and her mouth found its way back to Maple's. Her teeth closed over Maple's lower lip. Her tongue soothed the bite and slipped into the other woman's mouth.

A few pushes, some co-navigating while their tongues danced, and they were on the bed. Tali knew she wasn't going anywhere.

Their bodies rolled and roiled against one another, endless waves of need and want, directionless, driving them closer, closer, closer together. Tali wanted her hands everywhere on this body that was electrifying her own. She reached out and started unsnapping the straps on the overalls, only to have her wrists caught and pushed up above her head.

Maple was strong, holding both of Tali's wrists with one hand as her other palm slid along the side of the trapped woman's body, teasing and taking her time. All the while, they kissed with tongue and teeth and fathomless want. After an eternity, she got to where Tali's shirt tucked into her pants, and she pulled it free. Her fingers on a clear path to get under her shirt and—

Tali pulled her wrists as she removed her mouth from Maple's, the latter letting her go and sitting up, away.

"What's up?" The artist's eyes were hazy, her voice rough.

"Are you trying to top me?" Tali asked, suspicion lacing her tone.

"What? Yes, obviously. I'm literally on top of you." Maple laughed, her expression clearing. And it was true, in all of their rolling about, Maple had ended up on top of her, straddling her hips, holding her down.

And I liked it. Tali shook her head and sat up a bit more without dislodging Maple.

"Were you going to ask?"

"Uh, to top you? Should I have?"

"Yes! I'm a top."

"Are you?" Maple's playful expression suggested she knew how much Tali had been enjoying being held down. "Like, set in stone? You don't want me touching you? I should be good and keep my hands to myself while I let you fuck me?"

"Well, yes," Tali said, attempting to summon up some assertive tone to her voice. "I mean, no, I'm not a stone top. But, like, being touched is too intimate. I don't let that happen willy-nilly."

"Willy-nilly," Maple repeated back. "What a sexy word."

"You tease too much," Tali said, her face heating.

"Oh, I think I tease you just enough," she replied, a dangerous look in her eye. "In fact, I think you could use a lot of teasing."

"Uh." Tali gulped and had to fight to keep eye contact with the woman above her. She would have sworn Maple hadn't moved at all, but there was something new and hard in the other butch's posture.

Something that made Tali very wet.

"But," Maple said, voice light, "I, of course, respect your boundaries above everything else."

"Great, then let's switch positions."

Tali wanted this woman beneath her, wanted to grind into her hips and take her nipple between her teeth and teach her a lesson for all the teasing she'd done. She put her hands on Maple's hips to start rolling them over, but again the artist caught her hands and held them.

"Oh, I would," Maple continued in that playful tone of hers, "but I *am* a stone top, so however will we make this work?"

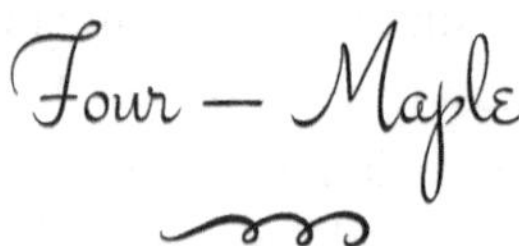

Four — Maple

Maple watched as the look in Tali's eye went from hopeful and horny to pure sexual frustration. It lit her up like a firework. She knew she shouldn't be enjoying fucking with this butch so much, but she did.

Tali was so wound-up she might snap. Maple was determined to be the one to help her uncoil before that happened.

"Are you fucking with me?" The woman beneath her asked.

Maple pressed Tali's hands into her hips, holding them there as she started to roll them against Tali's own.

"No, not fucking *with* you, but I'd like to *be* fucking you," Maple laughed. "Short of that, we'll have to find some sort of compromise, don't you think? What a tragedy, two tops, one bed. Nothing to be done about it."

"Yes, tragedy," Tali licked her lips, eyes roaming over Maple's body, clearly affected by the movement between their hips.

Maple let go of Tali's hands to lean over her, hands bracketing either side of her head, lips a breath away from another soul-snatching kiss.

"You're of course welcome to stay the night." Her voice barely above a whisper. "I can be a perfect gentleman, if you can."

"I hate you," Tali said back without a single ounce of sincerity in her voice. Her fingers still clenching Maple's hips.

"For respecting your boundaries?" Maple replied with mock confusion in her voice. "Or for offering you a place to stay?"

"You know for what." Tali almost moaned in response, her hips bucking up toward Maple in what seemed like an unconscious reaction. "I hope you're not lying just to get me to let you fuck me."

"I'm not a monster," Maple responded, her tone serious now, her body stilled. "I am who I am. And I'm not trying to fuck you anymore. But I *am* interested in teasing you until you come from sheer overload. How does that sound?"

Tali groaned and pulled a pillow over her face, mumbling something Maple couldn't make out for a moment.

"Although, I did have another idea," Maple said, letting the mischievous lilt back into her voice. "If you're interested."

The speed with which the pillow was removed proved that, yes, Tali was definitely interested. "What?"

"Well, we could both masturbate while you tell me what it is you would do to me, if I was open to you topping me."

With that, Maple leaned back on her heels, still straddling one of Tali's juicy thighs. The woman beneath her turned scarlet, though whether it was in embarrassment or desire, Maple had no idea.

Either way, it was fucking cute.

"Yes," was all Tali said for a moment and she pulled herself up onto the pillows behind her. She freed her leg from beneath Maple, swinging it around so that the kneeling artist was between her thighs now.

"Yes?" Maple started unbuckling her overall straps, eyes searching Tali's face for what came next.

"Are you comfortable with me watching you?" Tali asked as she unbuckled her own pants and slid them down a few inches, revealing the tops of boxers patterned with bulldogs.

Well, storing this image for future use.

"Yes," Maple breathed.

She got off the bed to shove her overalls and her bright orange briefs to the ground, yanking her t-shirt over her head. She climbed back on, naked except for her binder, and resettled between the other woman's legs. Her own knees were spread and she leaned back on her heels to give the butch a show. She was rewarded with Tali's groan, her head flopping back on the pillow, a hand rubbing over her eyes.

"Come on, little butch. Tell me how you'd fuck me."

There was that fire again. That immediate molten response to teasing. Tali's eyes bore into her own as the clothed woman slid a hand into her boxers.

"Well, I would have flipped you onto your back and removed those ridiculous overalls myself. And when you were as naked as you are now, I would have paid you back for all the teasing you've done tonight."

"Oh, how would you have done that?" Maple asked, sliding her fingers along the sensitive skin of her own inner thighs, shivering at the sensation.

"Fuck, you have beautiful hands," Tali growled. Maple watched Tali's wrist move in slow circles, imagined the path around a swollen, aching clit and wanted to follow suit. But she also was intrigued by this promise of teasing. "I would tell you to hold those hands still while I traced my fingers up your thighs like you're doing now."

"It feels so good," Maple shivered again. She was already so turned on. Had started this journey in the bar the moment Tali walked in with that swagger of hers. Had felt herself get wetter than she thought possible when they'd been kissing at the foot of her stairs and Tali's firm, masculine hands had gripped her hips. "It's almost too much."

"I'd keep doing that until you begged me to touch your pussy, and then I'd slide my fingers closer, but not close enough." Tali groaned and Maple desperately wished she could also see what Tali was doing, but didn't want to push her luck. Her extraordinary luck.

"Please, please," Maple mock begged. She could see that Tali knew she was just playing along, was yet again teasing her, but it still seemed to drive her mad. Oh this woman loved being teased as much as Maple loved to tease her. A dangerous combination.

"While I traced the edges of your pussy lips, I'd move my other hand to your mouth. Pushing two fingers in and watching you suck them. Get them nice and wet for me."

Maple did as the fantasy dictated, sliding the first two fingers of her own left hand into her mouth. Closing her eyes as she wrapped her lips around them and sucked. She let herself fall into the sensation, sliding her tongue along the ridges, slipping in between the fingers on her way back up to the tips. She slowly pumped into her own mouth, deeper each time. A moan surprised her as her other hand trailed across each of her soaked lips.

She opened her eyes, opening her mouth and sliding her fingers out along the length of her tongue. Tali had ceased moving. She seemed frozen in pure lust as she stared, fixated, on Maple's movements.

"Good girl," Tali rasped.

Normally that would have been Maple's line to say. Had always been Maple's line—except when it was 'good boy,' or 'good pet.' But something about them playing this out together felt right. Felt like a series of tiny fireworks going off from where her nipples pressed against her binder, straight to her clit.

"Now spread those pussy lips for me," Tali continued. "And let me watch you tease your hole with those dripping fingers."

And what could she do but listen to those words? Words that mirrored the thrumming desire in her own body. And she was glad she wasn't being told to touch her clit. She was afraid brushing it on her way to her entrance would be enough to make her explode.

Her fingers did their job too well and a raw, ravenous noise melted from the back of her throat. Tali groaned in response, her own hand back to its concealed work beneath those boxers. Maple wanted to taste those fingers, needed to know if this butch tasted as sweetly as she blushed.

Tali never moved her eyes from watching Maple's fingers circle and slide through her slick folds.

"How does that feel?" Tali's voice was still so stern, so direct.

"So good," Maple's own voice was dangerously close to a whine. This was more than she did with most partners, more than she'd let them see. But the way Tali looked at her, with worship in her eyes, it made her drip.

"Good, you've been so good for me." Tali's eyes took their time moving up her body, taking in the way Maple was thrusting against her own hand. Stopping on where Maple was pressing her teeth into her bottom lip, trying to keep from falling to pieces.

"Do you like to fuck yourself?" Her eyes were still on Maple's mouth. And so Maple released her own lip, tracing it with her tongue. Thinking again of how Tali would taste.

"Yes," she breathed.

"I want you to fuck yourself with as many fingers as you can take. Go slow so I can see your hungry pussy take every inch." That even, demanding voice. Maple was nothing but a puddle. "Can you do that for me, Maple?"

Of course she could do that. And she wanted to do it so well that Tali had no choice but to tell her she was a good girl again. So she did. Her right hand worked to hold her swollen lips open, her knees out as wide as she could manage. She positioned two fingers at her entrance.

Tali's heels hooked into the sides of Maple's hips, as if she wanted to pull her closer. Careful not to do anything the other woman might not be ready for, Maple dropped her pose and started to crawl forward. Tali seemed ready for it, adjusting so she could slide one thick leg between Maple's thighs.

Maple carefully leaned back again, rubbing her soaking wet lips and then her ass against the other butch's slacks.

And then her fingers were back where they belonged, teasing her entrance until her breaths were coming in gasps. She started to slide her two fingers into her, pausing for both Tali's benefit and her own sudden sense of it being too much. And not enough.

"More," Tali demanded, eyes never moving from the sight.

And that was enough to make it seem possible. She'd never liked being touched, wasn't interested in being touched in this way by other hands.

But being watched? She felt like she was on fire.

She pulsed her fingers in and out. So slowly. She watched Tali as she watched her. With each breath she pushed in a little deeper. And when she reached the last knuckle she slid out inch by torturous inch before adding a third finger and beginning again.

Tali seemed drunk with arousal. Her back came up off the mattress and she whined. *Whined.* Tough, severe Tali Blue was whining while watching Maple fuck herself.

"I want to come," Maple's voice echoing the raw need gnawing at her center.

"What do you need?"

"To rub my clit. Please."

"Do it, Maple. Be a good girl, show me how you like it." So assertive. *So fucking hot.*

She pulled her three soaking fingers from where they stretched her and slid them up through her folds to glide on either side of her clit. She bit her lip and moaned. It would only take a minute, she was so near to falling into the pleasure.

"Tell me when you're close," Tali demanded.

Maple wanted to close her eyes, to live deep in this feeling of the edge of collapse. But she wanted to see Tali's eyes on her more. Hungry, gray eyes sliding up and down her cunt, mapping out where Maple brought herself to ruin.

She skated her fingertips up and down the hood, little more than a suggestion of touch. And yet, she could feel the pressure building, knew it was around the corner.

"I'm so close, Tali."

"Come for me. Do it now."

And she did. Her eyes slammed shut, those fireworks that had been lighting up her abdomen now playing out across her vision, shooting through every nerve in her body.

She let herself fall, gasping, forward. She caught herself on her forearm, leaning just over Tali's body.

"Fuck," the butch beneath her groaned. "Holy fuck that was so hot."

"Your turn," she panted.

"Are you sure? You seem a little—"

But Maple met her eyes, attempting to replicate that sternness that seemed to come so easily to Tali. And then Maple slowly, extravagantly, licked around the ring of her lips and offered her open mouth.

Tali's brows lifted, but she slid her hand free from her boxers, from underneath Maple, and fed them into her waiting mouth. Maple moaned in gratification as she closed her lips and trailed her fingers through the exquisite taste of Tali.

"Suck," Tali commanded.

And so she did. She flicked her tongue under them, using the tip to trace the underside as her lips worked themselves deeper over them.

Maple worked her knee tighter between those gorgeous legs, pressing up against a warm center. She felt dizzy with her own orgasm, with the nearness of this other butch body, with her own daring exposure. Tali jolted, but then squeezed her legs tight, reaching around to grip Maple's hip with her free hand.

She began to ride.

Oh, how sweet it would be to truly top this woman. To make her come again and again. With her fingers, her tongue. To hear those whines and moans caused by Maple's body.

Fuck whatever she'd promised about being professional. There was no turning back from this now that she knew Tali tasted like citrus and called her dirty names. Not when there was a whole world of sensation they'd yet to explore.

Maple sucked with each thrust of Tali's hips, matching her beat for beat. The fingers pushed as deep into her mouth as they could go and Maple felt certain that Tali was feeling what she was. That this was more than either of them had ever hoped, and that it was nowhere near enough.

When Tali came she babbled incoherent words of praise and lust. She looked up at Maple with heavy eyes, pulled her into a sweet, languorous kiss, and then turned over. Maple fit herself to Tali's back, trailing her fingertips along her side as she felt her breath deepen and slow.

We're screwed.

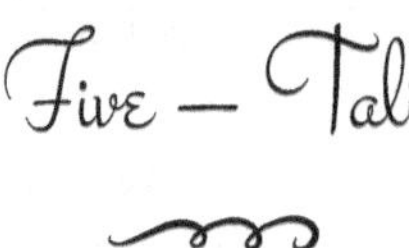

Five — Tali

Fucking shit. I mean, really, I'm definitely too old to be letting my "needs" lead me into stupid decisions.

"You alright over there?" Her sleeping companion asked from beneath an unbelievable number of comforters. Good thing too, since the room was freezing and also Tali was certain that if she saw Maple's muscular, soft, warm body she'd fall right back into bed with her instead of continuing to pull on all of her clothes. "It's still pretty early and I know for a fact that your meeting isn't until 10."

Tali ignored the wink the woman sent, along with the teasing words, ignored the flipping of her stomach. *Ugh, wow, just two coworkers.* She felt certain this was what mortification felt like, even if she'd avoided it until now. *How will I explain this to Simon. Or, oh shit, my sister?*

"Yeah," she said, her voice more tense, and way more honest, than she'd like. "Figured I should get some work done and review my notes before, uh, well, before we meet again."

"We could do that together, after a bit more time in bed," Maple patted the mattress next to her, her voice dripping with her meaning. "And I could take you out for breakfast to thank you for showing me such a good time."

Tali couldn't tell if she hated this woman and her blinding confidence or was in awe of her. It didn't matter, she had to set some boundaries now. Boundaries that should have been drawn last night, regardless of what the two of them were engaged in.

The sexy, mind-blowing things they'd engaged in.

"No, I don't think so. And I'd prefer if we could find our way back to being work acquaintances." Tali was a coward, she was sure of it. She was sure that this would be one of the moments she played on the shame projector in her head when she struggled to fall asleep and instead fell into endless embarrassment. "Last night was regrettable."

Something that might have been shock, and not a little hurt, covered the artist's features before she flipped over to drag herself up to a seat.

"Sure, work buds, got it. I'll see you out, good encouragement for me to do my run earlier anyway."

"You're going to go on a run?" Tali asked despite herself. *Oh, now you want to chat with this woman?* "After last night?"

"Last night wasn't exactly acrobatic," Maple laughed, but it didn't sound like her laughter from the night before. It wasn't teasing or joyful or free. In fact, it sounded less like laughter and more like the digging of a moat between them. "And let's not talk about last night, alright? I had a lot of fun, and I don't do the regret thing, but I'm also not going to tell you how to feel. So, let's leave it behind us and I'll see you at the apiary at ten."

Wow, good job, Tal, made a friend for life, didn't you?

She kicked herself mentally over and over again at her word choice and thought about how cathartic it would be to kick herself right there, in real life. *Or to let her punish me.* No, she couldn't be thinking things like that! *She* was the one trying to set boundaries.

"Alright, sounds good," she said, pulling on the last of her clothes and glancing over to see Maple already dressed in tiny running shorts and an electric blue sports bra.

Look away, Tali Blue. You just gave up any ability to admire how fucking good that woman looks in neon colors.

They walked back down the stairs in silence. The memory of climbing those stairs, of feeling brave and scared and, more than anything else, excited, rushed back to her. She'd been pretending to be the person she'd always wanted to be last night. Assertive, spontaneous, *sexy*. And now, here she was, back to being herself. So concerned with doing "the right thing," even when she had no idea what that thing was.

She wondered if she turned around right now, apologized for being an asshole, if that would be enough to set them back on a path more exciting than this one. Then again, there was the fact that she was pretty sure she could never live up to Maple's easy charm and constant teasing flirtation. The woman had no fear it seemed.

Be brave. You're not the person everyone thinks. You're not stuck.

So, on the last step of the stairs, before they'd be released out into the world where everything was too real and she'd lose her nerve, she turned around to say sorry.

And Maple, who had been stomping around behind her, lost in her own thoughts, didn't notice she'd stopped. Their bodies slammed into one another.

Tali fell hard onto her ass on the linoleum a step below her, sprawling across the landing as Maple flailed above her. The artist seemed to be desperately trying to not land on top of Tali, and then failed miserably.

They both grunted and groaned, Tali pushing at Maple's

body so she could get some air into her winded lungs. Maple struggled to her feet, already laughing and talking.

"What the hell, Tali?" Maple made it to a steady stance and stuck out her hands to help Tali up. "Are you trying to kill us both?"

"Me?" Tali asked, astounded. "You just walked straight into me! Do you ever look where you're going?"

Maple was quiet for a moment as Tali pushed her hands away and struggled to her feet on her own.

"Well, I was trying to be respectful," Maple said.

"Respectful?" Tali ran her hands over her butt, already feeling where the bruise would be later. "By pushing me down some stairs?"

"By not staring at your ass!" Maple was laughing again, but also unlocking the door and ushering Tali out. "You've made it clear you're not interested, but your ass is still perfect. So, I was doing the right thing and looking elsewhere. Not my fault you decided to take a little break on the last step with no warning."

Tali felt her face grow hot. Her ass? After everything she'd said, this woman was still interested in her in any way? Was she a glutton for punishment? Either way, it didn't matter. This did not bode well for a working relationship. She was beginning to wonder if they'd have to find another artist for this project. *Anna is going to be so mad.*

"Well, see you in a bit," Maple said, her voice still light, but now that Tali had heard how it could sound, she knew there was a careful distance there too.

"Yeah, see you."

Six — Maple

Well, what did you expect, May?

"Some human decency after a fucking good time," Maple answered herself out loud as she jogged in place to warm up her body. It was too cold for the run she was planning, but she'd do it anyway. She'd just have to warm up for longer.

As she felt the blood start pumping she couldn't help but replay that morning over and over in her head. How disappointing Tali's response to her had been, how it seemed to be fucking with Maple's own insecurities in a way she knew wasn't fair to put on the other butch.

So, she decided to replay the night before instead. Tali might be swimming in the depths of regret and self-hatred, but that didn't mean she needed to. As she ran over empty roads and past dewy meadows, she remembered the feeling of the other woman's soft hips under hers, the way her pupils seemed to take over those stormy eyes when she touched herself in front of Maple. The hope she'd allowed herself to feel that they could keep doing this until Tali felt safe and good enough for Maple to be the one making her gasp.

No, that was more than enough of that. Sure, she didn't

need to wallow in self-pity, but she also didn't need to lead herself straight to heartbreak by believing there was still any possibility of more.

Last night was fun. She'd had one night stands before. Normally she didn't have to keep seeing those sexual partners in a work context for months afterward, but they'd make it work. Because she was going to take this job, was going to prove she was the right artist.

The look on Tali's face this morning flashed into her mind again. Disappointment, embarrassment, incredulity. "Regrettable," rang in Maple's ears over and over.

And the burning word underneath was "unprofessional." All of Maple's desire to unwind whatever was keeping that rabbi so wound-up evaporated. She could keep her self-obsession and clenched shoulders. She wanted a collegial working relationship and to utterly ignore the fire ignited between the two of them last night? Fine.

And "professional?" Ugh. Code for "exactly the white, heteronormative standards that make me comfortable."

She ran past a cute little coffee shop that looked like one single customer could squeeze in at a time and reminded herself that Tali hadn't *actually* said the word professional.

This was the way in she'd been looking for after so many rejections from Jewish institutions looking down at her unorthodox—*no pun intended*—methods and upbringing. Organizations that only centered Ashkenazi work and told her to apply for Sephardic Heritage Month programming. As if that's where her identity and her work belonged—shoved into a one-month-long box and quiet the rest of the year.

No, she couldn't walk away from this opportunity.

And it definitely had nothing to do with the memory of Tali Blue's thighs pushing up against her.

Seven — Tali

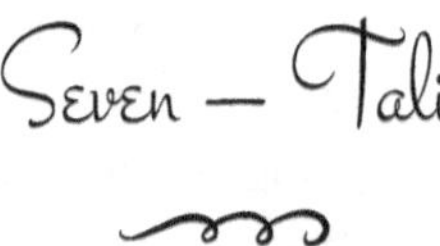

Maple was already waiting for her where the parking lot met the path when she pulled up before ten. The artist had changed into a floral button-up and slacks, a tawny coat hiding those muscular arms from view. Her hair looked wet and was unbound, trailing in tight curls to just below her shoulders. Tali couldn't help but think about how cold her head must be with its shaved sides, with no hat, wet. She thought about offering her own hat and then remembered how they'd left things that morning.

So, instead, she was totally normal and casual. She walked straight up to the taller woman, stuck out her hand and said, "You must be Maple, I'm Tali Blue."

Maple eyed her for a second and then laughed, putting her own bare hand in Tali's mitten, shaking it with a firm grip. "Rabbi Blue."

Tali blinked, but didn't correct her, and they went on to make small talk about Maple's run and the funky little coffeeshop Tali had found on her drive. When they ran out of topics, they stood in silence for a moment, absolutely being normal and pretending the previous night hadn't happened, waiting for their bee guide to show up.

"So, welcome to BEEPoRN."

"Uh, what?"

"That's the name of this place, BEEPoRN."

"No it's not," Tali argued. She had driven past the sign moments ago, framed by tall evergreen bushes, and was certain she'd remember if that was the name painted there.

"Well, fine, it *was* the name." Maple looked up at the sky as if reading the full name in the clouds. "Beatrice Elizabeth Engel Pollinator Research Naturescape. B-E-E-P-R-N. You have to assume that when her kids set up this place they *wanted* it to be called BEEPoRN."

"Oh. You *have* to assume that? That they wanted their mother's legacy to be a joke?'

"Man, you really are tied up inside, huh? Fun, Rabbi. Sometimes people like to have a little fun. And yeah, I do think it's a safe assumption. Who says 'naturescape'?"

"Hmmph." Not only was Tali entirely unwilling to cede that point, she was annoyed. Fun! She could be fun. Her entire job was to be fun with the teens. Well, and educational.

"Anyway, funders didn't love that people called it that for some reason, so they renamed it The Beatrice Pollinator Research Garden and Habitat."

Just when she was certain that she was about to say something else ridiculous in response to Maple, a heavily tattooed and underdressed queer came bounding up to them.

"Hiya, folks! You must be that rabbi Maple told me was coming, I'm Ollie." They stuck their hand out for Tali to shake and as she reached out her own, she noticed the tiny bee tattoos on their inner wrist. *Cute.*

"Does no one like to be warm up here?" She asked, releasing their hand. Ollie and Maple exchanged a look very much like rolled eyes. "And I'm not a rabbi, but I am here about Jewish things."

Maple's attention was suddenly entirely on her. A look of confusion clear across her features. *Now is not the time,* she tried to communicate back with her own eyes.

"Okie. Well, welcome to The Beatrice." Ollie, to their credit, didn't ask about it either, just nodded and conducted an exaggerated bow while they waved them onto the path, pointing out what would start growing soon.

It had been a cold year, so the ground looked mostly dead, but they reassured her that it was a full native plant wonderland for all of the warmer months.

"It seems like it's a lot of trees. Not as many meadows as I expected," Tali pointed out as they rounded the bend into another field full of them. There were several large greenhouses in the open field opposite, and a few small, elegant buildings farther along down the walk. She could tell that it would be breathtaking once everything woke from its winter slumber. Even now in the grossest part of the year, when everything was melty and muddy and brown and gray, it was beautiful.

"Yes!" Ollie turned around enthusiastically, gesturing at the trees with both arms. "Did you know that bees get most of their nectar from trees? These trees all bloom, and each tree provides thousands of blossoms for pollinators. Also, bees build houses from trees just like we do. Leaves and the resin are nesting material for bees, *and* there are plenty of pollinators that rely on holes in the wood for their homes."

Tali was honestly impressed. Not only with the facts, which she was surprised to realize interested her, but in Ollie's delivery. It was clearly a Tree Statement, something they probably had to memorize in training, and it also felt a little like the way Tali would write something for a children's program. But

Ollie delivered it with so much honest joy that it felt like a secret being revealed to her and Maple.

She snuck a look over at her walking companion to find her also smiling in response to Ollie's teaching, though she'd probably heard it several times before.

She was definitely starting to see why Maple loved it here so much. It was so peaceful and everything Ollie had been sharing was so important, so real. She'd never thought of herself as a particularly creative person, but even she was feeling inspired to create something.

"I can't wait to see all this when spring has actually shown up," she said without thinking.

"Oh, so you're sold on my idea then?" Maple's voice was so close to how it'd been last night—light, mischievous. "A Save the Bees campaign?"

"I didn't say that." Tali kept her own voice measured.

"Mmm, so you're going to reject my excellent idea, but then still come back to my sacred bee place?"

"Well," Ollie interjected, "obviously anyone is welcome. And we don't only support bees, wasps are excellent pollinators, as are—"

The look Maple shot them halted them mid-sentence. Instead, they smiled a knowing smile—*what do they know!*—and trotted off down the path to give them some space.

"I didn't say that either," Tali responded as if there'd been no interruption. "All I was saying was that I want to see how beautiful this place is when it's not still somehow winter."

"It's definitely spring now," Maple countered.

"I feel like..." Tali took a deep breath. "You're trying to rile me up at this point."

"Oh ba—I mean, oh, colleague, I've been trying to rile you up since the moment we met." That smile, almost too wide with perfect too white teeth behind perfect, kissable lips.

Stop looking at her lips! And what had she been about to say? Babe? Or, much worse, baby?!

The most annoying thing, Tali was certain, was that Maple must know how embarrassed she was, but she was refusing to acknowledge it.

Tali, after spending the whole morning driving aimlessly around this nowhere town, kicking herself for her own utter lack of professionalism in *sleeping with a colleague*, was now peeved that Maple was, well, so professional.

Until now.

"You were doing a great job," she heard herself say, as if from a great distance. "At the forgetting part, I mean. The, uh, I mean, moving from last night to being coworkers part. A great job."

Maple turned her laughing, sunny face to Tali—who had to fight to not look away from how infuriatingly attractive it was—and raised an eyebrow.

"And you've been doing a spectacularly terrible job at it."

Tali flushed, turning her attention back to the green-houses, fields, and hives around them.

Searching for my dignity.

She had no idea how this woman had lodged herself so far under her skin so quickly, or if she had done it intentionally at all. She realized how much worse that would be, if Maple was truly unaffected by her, was honestly totally over their night together, and their proximity meant nothing to her.

But, why? Isn't that what I want?

"Well then, you do remember last night?" *Oh, Tali, why? Why must you keep opening your mouth?*

"Don't be ridiculous." Maple snorted. "Duh. I'm, once again, trying to respect the boundaries that *you* set. Something you seem to dislike for some reason."

Tali felt her face heat, not because of the reminder of her boundaries last night, but because this near-stranger was right.

She had always been bad at enforcing her own boundaries, and now that someone was respecting them? It was weirdly intoxicating.

"Okay, well, that's..." she trailed off, at a loss for casual words that would convey her strange mixture of gratitude and discomfort. "But about the project, I still don't understand how you're proposing turning a Save the Bees campaign into an art thing."

"Swift topic change." Maple didn't press her further. She turned a bit away from Tali, looking over the grounds again. "Did you look at the portfolio I sent to Anna?"

"Yeah, of course I did." Tali had at least glanced at the site, but art had always been Anna's thing and she trusted her sister.

"Then you know my art is usually also a political campaign, or an educational experience. I'm not going to just take a picture of honey and hang it up in your boring temple lobby."

"Well, I can think of some old ladies who would be positively delighted by a large, beautiful honey picture in our boring lobby."

"I'm sure you can. But this would be a scandalous photo of honey if I had any say. So, the young queers might be *positively delighted*, but those nice, old ladies? Only some of them."

"How can honey be scandalous?" Tali asked, laughing despite herself.

Without moving, Maple slid her gaze along Tali's body, biting her bottom lip before answering.

"Well, Rabbi, I can think of a few ways. Want me to show you?"

Tali felt her face go autumnal red despite the spring chill. She spluttered out a few sounds of indignation, but Maple took mercy and began to lead them further along the path, following where Ollie had skipped off to a large, plain building. It wasn't an ugly building, but it certainly stood out against the exquisite beauty of everything else around it.

"I'm putting in a bid to do a collage." Maple inclined her head at the side of the building as they kept walking toward it. Calmly, cooly, as if she hadn't lit a match inside Tali.

She was toying with you. Which you probably deserve, after your performance this morning.

"On the brick?" Tali asked. She could be as cool. Probably.

"Yeah, I think they know it's not great looking, so they put out a call for bids. Seems like they won some beautification grant or something."

"That's cool, what are you—"

"Oh, hey there folks!" Ollie's chipper tones floated back over to them. "I see you found your way. So, Tali, here we are in the honey house. We don't actually have as many honey bees as folks think because they're actually not great pollinators compared to other types of bees. But, honey is the money maker! So, we do keep some honey hives, a bit further afield with their own pollination radius of gardens so there's no ickiness with the pollinator populations we try to cultivate here. And we buy honey from other beekeepers in the state to package and sell in our store. That's what funds about half of the operation."

"And the other half?" Tali was struggling to take in all the different stations around her. There were shelves of product, coolers in the back, work stations that looked like a huge industrial kitchen, and a long table with a few bins that held shallow amounts of honey in each.

"Oh, donations, grants. Our fundraising committee gets up to all sorts of things too."

"And what's this table of honey just sitting out?" Tali pointed at the bins.

"That's discard. Honey that wasn't good enough for whatever our team was putting together and it's hard to get out of the bins, so we set them there for the clean-up crew."

"Fun job," Maple commented, sounding genuine.

"A sticky job." Tali shivered. She hated the sensation of gooeyness. In fact, hated the texture and taste of honey. Her mother had always sworn by it, serving her orange pekoe tea with heaping spoonfuls of honey whenever Tali had a cold. She'd always taken one sip and gagged, refusing to drink the rest.

They toured the building, Maple pointing out all of the ways she imagined bringing this to life at Rosh Hashanah. And they were good ideas. Tali could admit that. At least, to herself. To Maple she found a lot of different ways to say 'maybe.'

In one corner of the building they met Ria, who hand-made birthday candles from the beeswax of abandoned bee hives.

"These are beautiful," Tali told her. They were simple, but after the dipping process, Ria carved tiny bees into each one. "This would be so great to have as Shabbat candles. Could you make them like this big?" She indicated with her fingers the approximate height and thickness. "I think they're called short tapers? They have to burn for more than four hours."

Ria handed her a business card and showed her a few more candle designs she'd done. Tali turned away from her smiling, only to meet Maple's smug gaze.

"See something you like?"

Tali's face heated at the double meaning and was about to say something else she'd probably regret when Ollie broke in.

"Okay, folks! That's pretty much the tour. I'll walk you back over to the entrance. You let me know when you'll be by again so I can make sure to say hi."

They were thanking Ollie and saying their goodbyes when Tali took a step backward, knocking into a shelf.

She twisted around to steady it. Immediately she knew her feet had betrayed her. Her right foot lost it. Her life flashed before her eyes as her arms pinwheeled, the last support of her toes sliding out behind her. She thought again of that smug look on Maple's face and fixed her mouth to curse her luck.

And fell face first into the discarded honey.

She truly could not believe her luck. Or rather, Tali's lack of luck. That was twice in one day that she'd watched this grumpy butch fall without an ounce of grace.

Maple fought to control her face muscles as Tali pulled herself upright and turned toward her. Her eyes were shut, her hands, dripping in honey, held up on either side of her head. Maple couldn't help herself, she pulled out her phone and snapped a photo.

"Am I dead?" Tali asked after working to pull her sticky lips apart.

Do not think about kissing those sticky, delicious lips. Do not! She disrespected you. And yet, Maple had recovered from that morning. The more time she spent with Tali, the more she realized that her reaction that morning had nothing to do with her, and everything to do with Tali's own fears and professional hangups.

"Um, hello?" Tali's voice edged on frantic this time and Maple realized she hadn't responded, and was still staring at this Creature from the Bee Lagoon.

"Hi, yes. I mean, no. You are not dead, just terribly

unlucky." Maple looked over to see why Ollie hadn't jumped in to help yet and watched as two tears streaked down their cheeks.

"Ollie, you okay, bud?"

"Is *Ollie* okay? Did *they* fall into bee discard?" Frantic was becoming shrill and Maple knew she needed to get Tali to a bathroom soon.

"Ollie?" She asked again, starting toward the crying queer. They pivoted their body on the spot, shaking with the tension of holding something back. But as soon as their eyes met Maple's they burst into laughter, clutching their sides and bending over.

"I'm so sorry," they said between huge gulps of air. "I was trying so hard not to laugh. It's not funny."

"It is *not* funny!" Tali echoed, cranking up the volume.

"Ollie, it is funny, but I have to get this not-rabbi to a private sink right now or she's going to explode all over the place."

Ollie took several more shaky deep breaths and then led them to the employee bathroom, Maple leading Tali gently by both elbows.

"I'm so grossed out," Tali admitted as she started trying to scrap the honey from her face with rough paper towels. "I hate honey."

"Honey's probably good for your skin."

"Maybe." She switched to trying a combination of warm water and what looked to Maple like rubbing it in. "I look like a PETA ad against bee abuse."

"Are vegans against honey? Are bees animals?"

"What? Were you listening to Ollie at all?" Tali moved her attention to her hands, clearly growing frustrated with paper towel bits ripping off and sticking to her hands. "Or are you one of those conspiracy theorists that thinks bees are robots?"

"I think that's pigeons. And it's this terrible lighting. You looked radiant out there."

Tali's hand stopped halfway back to her face for a moment before continuing on its journey. *Harder to tell if she's blushing under all that honey.*

"Plus, this is good to know. You have terrible taste and we could never be friends."

"You need more reasons we're incompatible?"

"It helps, the reminders."

"Oh, because I'm so irresistible."

Maple was sure Tali was rolling her eyes even while they were closed.

"Yes," Maple said. "Weirdly, you are. Must be your abundance of charm."

"I hate you."

"Doubt it." Maple laughed. "Anyway, want some help? I need to be heading back. I want to have plenty of study time tonight."

"You can leave me."

"Nah, I need to make sure I don't need to call some sort of hazmat clean-up squad."

"Fine. I'm just going to get as much off as I can with this sandpaper." She waved the paper towels in the air. "And drive home with this. A six hour organic face mask."

"Perfect." Maple reclined across the slatted bench and watched Tali's slow progress with no small amount of amusement.

"What class?"

"Huh?"

"You said you wanted time to study. Are you in school?"

"Oh!" Maple sat up, a warmth radiating through her chest at the thought of the class. "No, but I've been studying Ladino."

Tali turned, clearly defeated by her attempts at clean-up,

tiny bits of beige paper sticking to her cheeks and forehead. She narrowed her eyes at Maple, which made an unfortunate squelching sound in the remaining honey on her temples.

"The language?"

"Yeah." Maple stood to join her in leaving the bathroom and collecting their coats for the walk back to the parking lot. "I've been trying to learn for the past few years."

"Isn't it like a dying language?"

"Ouch." Maple shook her head as they exited back onto the tree-lined path. "I mean, it's endangered, for sure. But I speak it with my nonna."

"That's cool." Tali sounded like she would have rather taken another dunk in the honey than admit that.

"Thanks," Maple said, ignoring the tone.

"Sure. I mean, I had to learn Hebrew in school and it was the hardest thing I'd had to learn. I'm still not great at it, to be honest."

"Is that why you're not a real rabbi?"

Tali shot her a scorching look, which was only half as effective when her face was still glistening.

"I don't want to talk about that."

"Okay, what if I tell you a secret?" Maple asked.

"Ugh, I love secrets," Tali grumbled. "Fine, but it better be good."

"I think it is. I've been, well, I'm..." Maple took a breath, unsure of the sudden nervous fluttering in her stomach. "I've been working on this series of paintings that features Ladino heavily in the composition."

"Honestly, I don't know anything about art, but that sounds great. Why is that a secret?"

"Everyone knows something about art." Maple was startled by Tali's admission. Who didn't like art? *Is that just an artist thing to think? Do I live in an art loving bubble?* "And, I guess, because I've had some rough experiences with Jewish programs shooting down my work unless it's for some diversity initiative. And this is something I'm doing just for me and my community and I want it to be big."

Tali quietly nodded in response for the length of a path.

"I'm sorry that's been your experience, Maple. I hope this is a gamechanger for you and that those places realize what they've been missing out on."

"Wow, the person under the prickles emerges!"

"Okay, okay, moment's over."

"Wait, were we having a moment?" Maple widened her eyes in mock innocence. "I take it back, let's keep having it."

They'd reached their cars. Maple leaned against the grill of her hand-me-down, rust orange pick-up truck. Tali hovered anxiously in front of her own beat up gray car with a Frankensteined blue bumper.

"There wasn't a moment," Tali said. "And if there was one, you ended it. So, have a safe drive. I'll call you when I've talked to my boss and decided if we should do this."

"Tali," Maple said seriously, not moving from where she leaned. "I want this. I want to do this."

"Okay, I hear you."

"No, I mean it. It feels like you don't want this to work out. I keep giving you golden ideas, and you're shooting them all down."

"Feels like a lot of variations on the same idea."

"Yeah, well, even if that's true, it's the right one. Global warming and shit, so what's the problem?"

Tali looked torn for a minute, her lips twisting up in an unreadable expression, her hands finding purchase inside her coat. Maple wondered if the honey was freezing. It didn't feel *that* cold outside, but what was the freezing point of honey? Would it harden? Crystallize? *What would it be like to lick it off of her?*

"I'll admit to being a tiny bit resistant." Tali shifted from one foot to the other. "Anna, who emailed you, is my little sister."

"Uh huh."

"And this is her project to prove to me, and to this German program, that she doesn't need to go to college."

Maple studied Tali in a new light. Her voice was different, warmer, when she talked about her sister.

"And you want her to go to college?"

"I want her to have options." Tali toyed with her car keys. But it seemed more like a reaction to vulnerability than a desire to stop talking. "I want to help her. Maybe this is the right way to help her."

"Is it just you two?"

Anything to keep this softer version talking. It was intoxicating. She knew she should be building some emotional walls against Tali. If one of her friends was in her place, she'd tell them to run. But she wouldn't understand the vibrations that still felt like they were coursing through her body. The sheer amount of energy that pulsed between them the night before.

"No, Beth too. She's the middle sister. And our grandparents."

But no parents? It felt risky to ask anything that big in this surprising moment and she was saved by Tali's return question.

"What about you?"

"I'm also one of three sisters." She hesitated before adding, "but I'm the youngest."

Tali groaned and threw her head back. "Of course you are."

"What is that supposed to mean?" Maple asked in mock indignation, but already knew the answer. Her whole life people had pointed out that she was the quintessential youngest child.

"You're so free."

It was the sweetest way anyone had ever reacted to Maple's birth order, even if it was said in typical grumbly Tali fashion. She thought about her desires from the night before, about unspooling the taut thread of Tali. She couldn't help herself, she still wanted that. "You could be too."

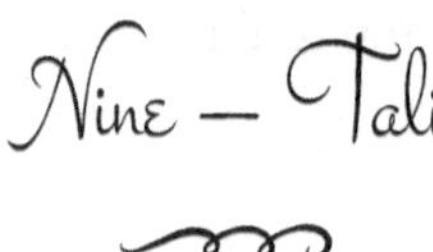

Nine — Tali

The phone kept ringing though she'd answered it multiple times in her dream.

"Shut up, phone." No, that didn't work either.

Finally she realized it was her real cell phone, really ringing, really early in the morning. After groping for it in the dark, Tali found her sister Beth's name on the too bright screen and groaned before answering it.

"Are you okay?"

"Wow, hi to you too." Beth laughed. Her sister was always laughing.

She's such a classic middle child. Always fun and funny, trying to keep people happy and engaged. Tali realized she might be a bit grumpy and reminded herself that she loved her sister, even at six in the morning.

"It's early, Beth, that's all. What's up?"

"Oh! I always forget about timezones."

"I mean sure, that makes sense, you've only lived in Atlanta for two years now." That made her sister laugh again although Tali had no idea why.

"I miss your grumpy face so much."

"My face is only grumpy before the sun is up."

"Well, that's not true." Before Tali could protest, Beth moved on. "So, anyway, I'm moving home! And we won't have to worry about time differences anymore!"

Those words were a bucket of ice water, jolting Tali awake. She'd been worried about Beth living so far away and it was always—well, usually—the best when all three Blue sisters lived in one city. Some quiet voice in the back of her head reminded her that they still wouldn't be all in one city if she would go back to rabbinical school already.

But she'd grown accustomed to ignoring that voice.

"Beth! That's great news. I mean, I'm not sure what room you'll be in because I'm sure you don't want to share with me or Anna, but we'll figure it out. Maybe the garage could be—"

"I'm not moving back to the house, Tali." Beth's tone was clear that she thought Tali was being weird. "I'm an adult, I'll get my own place. And isn't Anna going to like Germany next year?"

"Anna *might* be going to Germany. Otherwise she's going to a state school, and I imagine still living at home. At least the first year." She took a steadying breath, pulling herself out of bed. "And I am also an adult, Beth. There's nothing wrong with moving back to the house. It'll help you save some money while you look for your next job."

"I'm moving back because I *have* a new job. I got the wildlife conservation position." Her voice was so full of joy that she practically squealed. Tali's own pride in Beth's success was almost enough to take the sting out of her sister's next words. "And Tal, there *is* something wrong with moving home if you get stuck there."

Ouch. But there was no reason to tell her sister how sharp those words landed. No reason to create any more distance between them. It was always easier with Anna, who'd been only ten years old when their mom died and Tali moved home.

Beth had been a teenager, practically grown. And she'd had the hardest time dealing with the grief. She hadn't wanted to go to the therapist that Tali had found for all three of them. Had been furious when Tali moved into their mother's room.

They'd made it through, somehow, over the last seven years. The last two in particular, while Beth had pursued more vet tech training, rather than follow Tali's route to college, had proved healing. Maybe the distance had been the best thing. Maybe she should be more worried about her moving home.

She couldn't bring herself to feel that. She loved her sisters so much that it felt like too much to look at straight on. And they were adults now. This would be good.

And it only hurts because you want to go back. Tali shut that thought up by returning to the more pressing issue.

"So, when are you moving back?"

"This summer! I should be back in time for the family bbq." Meaning Fourth of July, but since her grandparents were far from being patriots, they'd never called it that. They called it Family BBQ Day and ignored all the flags and fireworks their neighbors shot off, often handing out political pamphlets to friends they thought could use some education.

"Do you need help apartment hunting?"

"No, I know you're busy. High Holidays, Jewish teens needing discipline, Anna not going to college, blah blah."

"Again, Anna is *going to college*, or that German program which is sort of college."

"You should talk to her about that," Beth said, her voice hinting at some sisterly secret Tali had been left out of. *Fine. Time to open up that conversation with Anna again. Fun.*

"So how are you finding an apartment then?"

"Maddy is looking for me. She's going to video call me when she finds a good one and that'll be that."

Maddy, Beth's best friend, had so clearly been in love with Beth since they'd met in Girl Scouts as kids. Tali often wondered if Beth knew that. What she did know was that above all else Beth hated meddling, or being helped in any way. So, she kept her mouth shut.

"No one needs me anymore, huh?"

"Tali, you've been a great sister-mom. It's time you're just a sister."

Tali stomped to the kitchen an hour later to find her grandmother lovingly running a soft brush over Anna's shaven head.

"Morning," she mumbled as she bee-lined to the coffee. Her grandfather beat her to it, pouring her a huge mug of it and kissing her cheek as he handed it to her.

"Good morning, our favorite Tali," her grandmother said, taking a seat next to where Anna was scarfing down pancakes.

"Pancakes?" Tali looked around the kitchen to find evidence of the morning's meal.

"I ate 'em all," Anna said around a mouthful.

"What!" Her stomach rumbled in time to underline her disbelief.

Her grandmother clucked her tongue and tapped the teen on the shoulder with the brush. "Anna, don't tease your sister. You know she's not a morning person. They're in the microwave, sweetheart."

Tali retrieved them, along with cream cheese and jelly from the fridge, and began to construct her pancake rolls.

"What's the special occasion?" She asked after her first bite and profusely thanking her grandmother for the delicious surprise.

Her grandfather shuffled out of the room, probably out to

his tinkering shed, as her grandmother took a seat across from her. Tali loved them so much she thought her heart might burst. The Blue sisters had always lived with them, their mother had never left home. There'd always been someone home to help with homework or take them to rehearsals and practices. Her mother had been a big believer in communal living and in family units.

Tali was especially grateful for that community now. She had been so overwhelmed with gratitude for their home when her mother had unexpectedly died those seven years earlier. So much of their mother was still around every corner. And her sisters hadn't had to deal with moving while they grieved.

Her grandmother's voice, increasingly gravely and worn in age, pulled her from her reverie. "Dear, you have some jam on your chin. And sometimes you feel like making pancakes."

"Well, I'm glad we benefited from your whim."

"And there is a lot to celebrate," Anna cut in as she took her dish to the sink and started washing it. "You met with that artist. I'm emailing her with my draft of the ritual today—"

"Anna," Tali tried to interrupt. She still felt uncertain. She thought Simon's council, or maybe just his reassurance, would make her feel ready to commit to working with Maple.

"And Beth is moving back! She called me this morning," Anna continued, ignoring Tali's interjection. "Did she tell you?"

"She did." *So early. Maybe that's why everyone's so awake right now.* "She also said something else to me."

Tali turned to watch Anna's back as her sister scrubbed the pancake pan. "What does Beth mean about you definitely not going to college?"

Anna froze, one soapy hand in midair. "Uh."

"Tali." Her grandmother had turned on her most diplomatic voice. It was the sound that reminded her most of the squabbles between Beth and Anna when they'd been younger.

Her grandmother would swoop in and make them explain why they were fighting and ask them to describe the situation from the other side. *Should have been a judge.*

"Okay. What's the secret?"

Tali's office was too quiet. It was cavernous, the rest of the morning's conversation playing on loop in her mind.

Anna had never actually applied to safety schools. She was only planning on this program and if that didn't work out then she was taking a gap year. Or not going to college at all.

In theory, Tali was all for people not going to college. Higher education was extremely classist and generally inaccessible. Beth was living an independent life filled with adventure without any traditional college education.

But she also thought about her own peers, about how hard it was for some of them to find jobs that paid anywhere near a living wage. With or without their college degrees.

They'd been so privileged in so many ways, but money was tight. Tali had worked throughout high school to help out, and that was before they'd lost their mom.

No. She wasn't going to despair. That was too easy. She would make sure Anna worked hard and did her best and had a real chance of going to this program. Of chasing her dreams.

She'd deal with their hurt trust and being lied to later.

> Tali: okay - send me those plans of yours
> again

> Maple: Look who it is!

> Maple: I was just about to email your sister.
> Want me to CC you?

Tali: Yes

Maple: Wordy, I like it.

Tali: Ugh

Maple: How was the drive back?

Tali: Fine. My ass still hurts from our stairs incident

Maple: I wish I'd made you sore from other activities

Tali: What

Tali: Why

Tali: Are you flirting with me just to piss me off?

Maple: Idk, does that do it for you?

Tali: What happened to us being colleagues?

Maple: I've been thinking

Tali: Well, that's an improvement

Maple: About us

Tali: Nvm, that's worse

Maple: And what I've decided is that I'm going to work on this project with Anna exclusively. Since it's her thing.

Tali felt a sudden, unwanted pang at that message. She'd known the flirting was to get under her skin. Maybe to pay her back for all her bullshit. And yet—

No, 'and yet' nothing. It was a one-night thing. Sure, she unlocked something in me that I desperately need to spend some time thinking about. But hey, sometimes that's just good sex. It works things loose. You're cool. You can be unattached and aloof.

> Tali: Great sounds good. I'll get your contract ready

> Tali: And then yeah, just CC me on the emails since she's a minor

> Maple: Perfect. And then you and I don't have to worry about being colleagues.

> Tali: Right

> Maple: So I can flirt as much as I want to

> Tali: WAIT NO

Tali *wanted* to focus on work. She had at least sixty hours of work to cram into her forty hour week with Passover right around the corner and her teens all having teen problems. But her ability to focus was entirely gone.

It has nothing to do with all this texting with Maple. They'd continued to text for a while after Maple's shocking message. They'd found their way from there to talking more about Maple's recent Ladino lessons and how her art was coming along.

But that was normal. It was fine. It wasn't distracting. No, she was a sensible person. She was having an off day. That was all. So, she decided it was a great time to unsubscribe from all the newsletters she was never going to read anyway. That lasted close to five whole minutes before deciding she'd go find Simon and ask to have their meeting a few minutes early.

After close to half an hour of searching the synagogue building, Tali finally found Simon in the kitchen.

"Uh, Simon?"

He jumped and spun around, cookie crumbs falling from his stubble and fingertips. Tali sucked her lips in to keep from laughing.

"Hmm?" At least, Tali assumed that was the sound he was attempting, though all she heard was air escaping through a mouthful of dry cookie.

"We were supposed to meet like ten minutes ago. I thought you'd fallen asleep while practicing your dvar again."

As soon as Simon finished chugging the glass of water he held in one crumby hand, he let out a sound of pure indignation.

"One time! *One* time you find me *taking a nap*. You act like I'm falling asleep all over town."

"Hey, no judgment. You're the rabbi here."

"Try this cookie." Simon fished one out of the white bakery bag and brandished it at her.

"Uh—"

"Come on, please. I obviously can't be trusted. I still think Mrs. McCutcheon's cookies are great." Simon put on puppy dog eyes to drive the request home.

"Si—"

Both of them swiveled toward the door as Larry, one of Tali's teens, attempted to back out of the room unnoticed and instead knocked over several folding chairs. Tali had two thoughts in quick succession. *What cruel parents named this kid Larry?* Which was her thought every time she saw him. And: *what trouble is he trying to get into?*

She decided she'd talk to him about it later when he wasn't looking so embarrassed.

"Hi, Larry." She put on her patient teacher's face as he waved his full arm in response. "Bye, Larry."

He took the hint and the opportunity to slink from the room.

"What is he doing?" Simon asked, still watching the door the kid had left from.

"I dunno," Tali admitted. "Give me this cookie."

After her full review of the cookie, which came from a new bakery in Simon's neighborhood—*sweet, maybe edging on cotton candy, but not dry*—they started the walk back to their offices.

"So, how was the trip to the artist?"

It had been on their check-in agenda. She knew Simon was going to ask her about it, even if she herself had not decided to put it on that agenda. And yet, she had no idea how to respond to the question. No matter how friendly they were, he was still her boss. And a rabbi. But rabbis had sex.

But, again, my boss, don't be weird.

"Tali? You're being weird. What's up?"

Damn it.

"How am I being weird?"

"Well, maybe you have to use the restroom? You're squirming a lot."

"Ugh, fine. The artist was fine. The trip was great. Bees are magical."

"Uh huh." Simon squinted, and his tone let her know he wasn't interested in the bullshit.

"How much information do you want?"

Simon's eyes went the way of saucers. Tali could only imagine what he was thinking. Before she could backtrack, they'd reached his office and he ushered her inside.

"Well." He took a seat and waved impatiently for her to do the same. "What genre of information are we talking here?"

And then it was as if all of the common sense in her head decided to take a hike.

"I slept with her but only sort of, because we're both

tops."

In the long, tense silence that followed, Tali wondered how long it would take to pack up her office. Was it as difficult as she imagined to create a new identity and start over? Perhaps this was finally the moment she decided to go back and finish school, simply to never have to face Simon again.

"Simon!" She finally couldn't take the silence any longer. She was certain she'd broken him. He hadn't moved except to close one eye and look at the ceiling with the other.

"I'm surprised," he said.

"There are tops and bottoms for lesbians?" The question came from the doorway. The open doorway. The doorway where Anna leaned against the jamb as if she too had been invited for this meeting.

"What!" Tali felt her jaw drop as she turned in her chair to face her sister.

"No!" Simon shouted at the same time. "Do not answer that. Entirely inappropriate. I think I'm in shock."

Anna plopped into the free chair, staring at Tali with both eyebrows raised.

"Well?"

"Well, what?" Tali shot back.

"Tops? Bottoms? What?"

Simon put his hands over his ears and shut his eyes. Tali wasn't entirely sure whether he was trying to block out the conversation or trying to wake up from this nightmare.

"Anna," she hissed. "We will talk about this at home. Where we will also talk about why you are here and not at school. Please—"

"It's practically graduation. And it's half day for service, Tal."

Oh, crap. She'd entirely forgotten that this morning when she couldn't focus long enough to read over her schedule. Maybe that was why Larry was there.

Anna shook her head at Tali's sheepish expression. She heaved the weary sigh of a teenager with the weight of the world on her shoulders and twirled out of the office, waving an enthusiastic goodbye to Simon.

Simon who had aged a hundred years in the space of that interaction.

"Sorry," Tali muttered. "I don't know what came over me."

"With the... the, uh, choice you made?" Both of them winced. "Or with telling me?"

"Both?"

"I see. Well, like I said, it is surprising." Simon sighed. "Because it's so unlike you to do anything—"

"So unprofessional?"

"For yourself," Simon corrected, a sad sort of smile flashing across his face.

"That's not true." Tali felt legitimately taken aback. He was supposed to be ashamed of her. She'd acted recklessly. *Shamefully.* "I leave work early once a month to go watch a movie!"

"Oh no! Watch out! A selfish monster's on the loose and it wants an hour or two alone every once in a while!"

Tali heaved a sigh and deflated in her chair until her head rested on the back of the seat.

"Tali, all I'm saying is that it's surprising. Not that I'm upset with you. I mean, we are friends, but please don't tell me about your sex life. That was weird." He shook his head as if to erase the words from his memory. "But if you liked this person, don't get in your own way."

"I didn't say *anything* about liking her."

"Fine, but I worry about you. About how much I've been enabling you. Are you not interested in her, or are you not interested in moving forward with your life?"

"Ugh, Simon. Why don't you stick to your cookie war?"

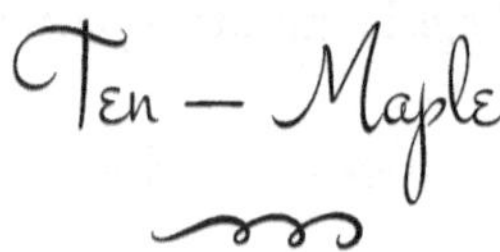

Ten — Maple

Maple had spent the morning creating more than she had in the last several months. *Maybe sex was the secret after all.*

She felt like a door had been unlocked inside of her. Between some commissions she had finally wrapped up, emailing with Anna some preliminary sketches for the Rosh Hashanah project, adding two new classes to her roster for the summer, and a full three hours of generating new ideas for the Ladino series, she felt like a rockstar.

Plus she'd spent weeks now flirting with Tali. It had been exhilarating. She had no idea where it was going, *if* it was going, but wow it had been fun. Tali, whose grumpiness seemed even sillier and cuter through text. Tali, who remembered small details Maple shared with her. Tali, who—*is texting me right now!*

Tali: okay, I need some info

Maple: Shoot

Tali: ??

Maple: As in - go ahead

Tali: oh

Tali: I need your last name, business
address, and hourly rate. I only have your
project rate

Maple: k

Maple: Pull. I need to figure out both those
other things since I just moved studios -
and I usually only charge by project - hold
please

Tali: Pull?

Maple: My last name

The three typing dots appeared and disappeared several
times to Maple's amusement.

Tali: Your name is Maple Pull?

Maple: No

Tali: WHAT

Maple: My name is Esme Pull

Tali: And "Maple"?

Maple: Is my name

The pause in texts was long enough that Maple started
doing the math on her hourly rate and looking up the address
of the studio she'd moved to the month prior when her phone
began to ring.

Tali's name appeared on the screen and Maple couldn't
stop the stupid grin from pulling at her lips.

"Rabbi Blue?"

"You think you're Cher?" The crisp agitation that had

come to define Tali in Maple's mind came through the phone clear as day.

"Cher who?"

"Exactly. I don't know Cher's last name—"

"Bono Allman," Maple offered. She was rewarded with a short huffing sound.

"Well, that's obviously not the point."

"Isn't it?" Maple was certain her ear to ear smile was radiating through the phone, which would only serve to piss Tali off more.

"No! It's not. The point is that you've made yourself a whole new name like you're a rockstar."

"Okay. Why don't you practice some calming breaths. Three points. One, it's called a nickname, Tali. Look it up."

"Hmmph."

"Two, what kind of queer are you? I can have a chosen name. Lots of people have chosen names."

"Again, that's not the point I was—"

"And *three*, I *am* a rockstar. It's so funny you said that because I was literally just thinking about that before you texted." Maple sat back in her chair to wait for what she was certain would be a series of undignified grunts.

"Are you? A rockstar?"

It sounded like a genuine question, which was so shocking that Maple pulled the phone from her ear and looked at the screen again to confirm that yes, still Tali.

They'd exchanged numbers before making their long drives back to their homes after BEEPoRN. In the intervening weeks, she'd found that Tali loved to text. But, even more, she loved to text in order to initiate a phone call. All of that had been a thrilling discovery, despite knowing it was a fruitless one. Tali Blue was likely never going to pull her head far enough out of her own ass for the two of them to have a real shot.

"Yes, I am, and you don't always have to be such a jerk."

"Was I being a jerk?" Another genuine sounding question from Tali. Maybe she'd had some sort of life changing experience recently.

"Did you go skydiving?"

"What the hell are you talking about?"

There she is. "Nothing, but yeah. You were being a jerk."

"Well." A puffed out breath of hesitation came through the speaker. "Sorry."

"I'll forgive you. Mostly because that sounded hard for you to say and I don't want you to pop a blood vessel."

"I hate you."

"Sure you do."

"It's just been a day." She could hear Tali moving some papers around and was reminded of why they'd started talking at all.

"Wait, I want to hear about your day, but were you texting me because I'm definitely in?"

"Unless you come back and tell me some sort of outrageous hourly rate, yeah. You're our artist."

Maple jumped up from her couch and shook her arms in the air, kicking her feet out like Snoopy, and narrowly avoided knocking over at least three cups of brush rinsing water.

"Did you hear me?" Tali asked, accompanied by more paper rustling sounds.

"Yes! Sorry, busy doing a happy dance over here."

"What does your happy dance look like?"

"I can promise nothing like what you're picturing." Maple flopped back on the couch, kicking her legs out a few more times for good measure.

"What do you think I'm picturing?" Even louder rustling now. It felt like Tali was talking to her from inside a paper bag.

"Something sexy." Maple dropped her voice, attempting something close to sultry. "And masculine. Like a scene straight out of Magic Mike. But I'm using my easel instead of a pole."

"I didn't watch that movie."

"Surprise, surprise." Maple made her voice clear that it was anything but.

"Whatever," Tali huffed. "I wasn't picturing anything."

"No need to lie, Tali. We're all colleagues here." Maple bit her lower lip to keep from laughing at her own joke. "Okay, tell me about this day you're having and how we can turn that around?"

Tali hemmed and hawed, the creaking of her ancient office chair coming through as a piercing punctuation mark in the conversation. "It's just these teens."

"Being teens?"

"Well, yes. But also wanting the world to be better. And I find myself caught between wanting to help make it better *for them*. And wanting to prepare them better. But that borders on crushing their spirits, and I can't."

"So, let's make it better."

"My delicate heart or the world?" Tali often got quieter when she was being vulnerable. It made some long dormant part of Maple ache.

"Both?"

"How?" Almost a whisper.

"Why don't you take them to BEEPoRN? And then help them do something like an education and neighborhood cleanup campaign?"

"That's not a bad idea—"

"What praise."

"Do you have a praise kink?"

"You want to know my kinks, Tali Blue?"

"But I definitely can't take them if you keep calling it BEEPoRN."

"It's the name, Tali!"

"No, no, it's not."

"You're no fun."

"Thank you." She sounded genuinely pleased.

A pattern surfaced. When they weren't talking, they were texting. When either of them had a long or hard day, they'd resort to mostly emojis and gifs. Tali still grumbled and bemoaned Maple's general existence. But more of the secret, soft, sweet underbelly was revealed.

She pressed send on a particularly lewd message, imagining the flurry of rageful but entertained texts soon to be headed her way, as she walked out into the classroom area of her studio. A sound in the corner had her suddenly alert, only to find her mother leaning against one of the desks. "Oh my god, Ma, what on earth?"

Her mother shook her head slowly, an amused look spreading across her lips. "Who are you texting, you look happy."

"Uh, it's a work thing." Maple lied, sliding her phone into her back pocket and staying in the doorway. The mental image of her mother reading that last text, or any of the texts, she sent Tali made her want to chuck her phone out into the street.

"That's all you ever do, work, talk about work, think about work. When will you date?"

"If this is another cry for grandkids, I'll say what I've said before: get off my back, I love you so much." She said it with as much deference in her voice as she could. She respected her mother deeply and wanted nothing more than to honor her and make her proud. But this kids thing was a hard line. "I'm the youngest, I feel like that should buy me some time."

"Oh, so you don't want me to have fulfillment in this life?"

They'd tread this same conversation so many times, Maple knew what her response was supposed to be. But she didn't want to humor her. She had no plans for children. She loved teaching them art, but she also loved sending them home at the end of the day.

"Ma, I think you need more hobbies. Me having kids is not going to cure your boredom, I promise."

"That's not what your father thinks."

Maple snorted. Her father seemed entirely indifferent to Maple's choices as long as they made her happy. "I doubt that."

"Fine." Her mother heaved a heavy sigh, but then let it slide completely away. A warm smile replaced the previous concerned lines. "Come here, let me hold my baby."

She walked across the room into her mother's open arms. She smelled like she always did, of lilacs. Her strong arms squeezed Maple in tight before spreading her hands across her back and rubbing gently until Maple was the one to step away. Like always.

"Okay, no more talk of babies," her mother said with a sharp nod. Her stylish asymmetric bob swung with the gesture, the light playing across the strands. She thought again about how she should convince her mother to let her paint her. "What do you want to talk about instead? Nonna tells me you're doing some Ladino art, let me see."

"Nonna is telling my secrets." Maple picked some lint off her mother's shoulder, but it was a pointless task. She was wearing a pure black sweater that seemed to be made entirely of lint. Far too hot for the season, but her mother was always covered up and usually in all black.

"No secrets in this family, my baby." The older woman reached up and patted Maple's cheek. "Come, show me."

Summer

FROM THE OFFICE OF THE BEATRICE:

Dear Flower Children,

Happy summer! Those of us here at The Beatrice can't wait to see you all at this season's classes. We're offering a lot of the classics, and a few thrilling new options. Sign up below!
[...]
Monthly fun pollinator fact: Making a *beeline* to the food table? Well, that's more than just a cute phrase and our bee-havior at every party. Tell a human and a computer to find the shortest route between multiple destinations and they'll both have to do some serious math.

But bees? They're the only animals that can figure out the most efficient path to multiple flower stops immediately!
[...]
So send us photos of those pollinators you attract to your yard this summer!

–The Beatrice Team

PS: To our very enthusiastic bee fans—please stop placing signs in front of our entrance sign using our outdated acronym: BEEPRN.

As a reminder, we changed our name several years ago to "The Beatrice Pollinator Research Garden and Habitat." Any former names may forever live on in our memories, but we'd like to avoid confusion by not alerting new friends of our previous name.

Eleven — Tali

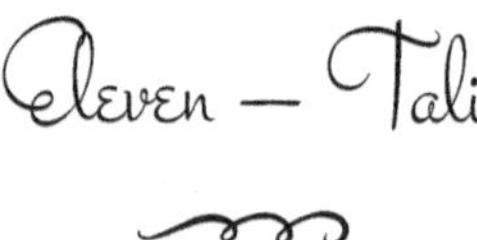

On a particularly hot day in June, Tali woke up with the bridge of her nose feeling viciously tight. She stumbled from her bed to the bathroom, ripping the drawers open and rifling through their contents. When she ran out of drawers, she turned her attention to the cabinets.

Anna found her an hour later, curled on the bathroom rug in total darkness. The bathroom opened on either side, into Tali's room, which had once been their mother's, and into Anna's, which all three girls had once shared. As her sister pulled the door open, letting in some of the morning light, Tali hissed like a boiling tea kettle and burrowed her face into her crossed arms.

"Tal," Anna whispered, closing the door behind her, stepping into the darkness with her. "Why are you on the floor?"

"My lane," Tali slurred, and Anna took a moment in silence, perhaps to piece together what those words meant. Eventually, she got it.

"Shit." Anna crouched, her eyes starting to adjust to the low light provided by cracks between door and jamb. "Where're your meds?"

Tali swung an arm at the open drawers and cabinets as if to say, *who the fuck knows*. Anna quietly left the bathroom without speaking again and Tali wondered if she'd leave her there to suffer forever. She probably deserved it, after all the grief she'd been giving her about going to college. But now wasn't the time to worry.

And it wasn't hard to push the thoughts from her mind. She was almost entirely preoccupied with the throbbing tightness of the migraine wrapping itself around her skull. Dipping its roots behind her left eye.

Anna came back, Tali couldn't tell how long she'd been gone. Time was funny when her migraines started. Anna was clearly trying to be as quiet as possible, but every sound felt like a punch to the side of her head.

"I'm back," she whispered, as if the world's loudest door hinges hadn't announced her presence. Of course she came back. Of course she'd found Tali's oh-no-the-migraine-got-in emergency pills wherever she'd left them the last time this had happened. *Silly to think she'd leave you here.*

Anna helped her sit up and take two of the pills with sips of water far too cold. Helped her stand on shaky legs and walk back to her room, where Anna had drawn down the blackout curtains. Tali gently dove beneath all of the blankets, took the ice pack headwrap from her sister and drifted right back off to sleep.

Tali woke up several hours later. *Still migraine. Ow.* But she ventured a look with one slitted eye at her phone screen to send two texts.

The first to Simon. After seven years of working together, they had a migraine code. "Mean brain."

He'd clear her schedule for her and email anyone who needed to be rescheduled. Sometimes he taught her classes for her, if he had a free hour. The teens always begged her to never let it happen again because Simon loved to teach ancient Jewish history, regardless of the actual topic of the class.

The other text was to Maple, in case Anna hadn't already let her know. They were all supposed to meet up at Maple's studio. There was a showing of student work and they'd decided to drop by during it to finalize the plans for the project.

She's going to think I'm trying to get out of seeing her.

But a text came back seconds later.

> Maple: That's awful. I'll reschedule with Anna. Do you want me to bring you anything? Soup? Some weed?

> Maple: And I'll give you a private showing anytime you want

After months of texts and calls, Tali knew that was meant to be sweet, but Maple couldn't help also being a little suggestive.

They all found a time that worked that weekend, so Anna and Tali drove up to the studio early Sunday morning. Early for Tali, at least. Anna was bubbling over with ideas and plans the whole drive up. She'd asked Tali to let her drive, but that was a bridge too far. Anna had passed her driver's exam after a full six tries. More contained, nonhighway practice was needed. *Maybe I'll make Beth take her driving when she gets here.*

The studio was on a corner of a street lined with cute, quirky shops. It was situated just over the town limits, beautifully framed as they rolled around a bend by the "Farlight Village Welcomes You" sign. The building looked plucked from the hillsides of Greece. It was two stories, stark white stucco with brilliant blue trim and plants growing in every window.

Maple was waiting for them in the doorway when they walked up.

"You own this whole place?" Tali couldn't stop her eyes from sweeping over it again, and then turning to look at the yarn store next-door and the bustling cafe across the street. Dogs and their humans frolicked in a park a block away *Idyllic. No wonder she's always so happy.*

Maple moved to wave them inside. Anna hopped in after her, clutching her notebook of last-minute ideas. Tali dragged herself away from the bright, Hallmark scene to follow. "I own this part of the building. The studio and the apartment above it. After my classes took off, I decided to put down roots and invest in the space.

"Is this where you grew up?" Anna asked as she set her notebook on the table they'd reached. They all chose seats, Maple's eyes on Tali's body as she settled into hers.

"No, but not far from it. My mom drives over often enough that I wonder if I should have picked someplace slightly farther away." She laughed, and Tali knew she was joking. She'd learned a lot about Maple's mother over the last few months. How smart and sweet and caring she was. How terrifying she could be when anyone hurt her children. It made her heart squeeze. A little jealousy, a lot of joy. "But there are a lot of bougie parents here who want their kids to be artists. So, good for me."

That set Anna off on a series of a hundred more questions. Maple took each of them seriously and answered them honestly. Tali leaned back and watched the conversation, waves of cool peace washing over her.

Finally it came time to review the plans. Maple stood and unrolled papers she poured out of a long tube.

"Okay, here they are," she said, standing back. "What do you think?"

Tali leaned closer to look. Then she stood up, placing her hands on the table and leaned even closer. *This is probably how it started for Simon getting too close to read things. I should get my eyes checked.*

But she realized her eyesight hadn't been wrong. The drawings of the lobby where the program would take place had been partitioned off into sections labeled "clown enclosure," "disco floor," "literal soapbox—made of soap," and other equally absurd ideas.

Tali spluttered and stood up, looking at Maple incredulously. "What is this? We haven't texted about *any* of this. It doesn't make sense."

"Texted?" Anna asked, a mischievous glint in her eye. "I thought you said all of this was up to me. Have you been checking up on me."

"No!" Tali felt her face heat, realizing there was no easy way out of this conversation.

"I mean, we haven't talked about Maple since the conversation with Simon—"

"Anna!" Now she was certain she would die right on the spot. She braved a look at Maple, only to find the taller butch biting her lip and laughing. "What's going on?"

Maple reached forward and pulled back the top sheet of paper to reveal the real plans underneath. "Your sister emailed me yesterday to ask if we could prank you, and of course I said yes."

Tali grumbled, retaking her seat and crossing her arms. "Not funny."

"I think it was funny." Anna laughed. "And wait, you two have been texting?"

"No," Tali said at the exact same time Maple was saying, "Yep."

Anna rolled her eyes and opened her idea notebook.

The meeting was coming to an end when a teen in an oversized tee and shorts, holding a neon pink skateboard, came into the gallery. Tali was certain Maple would tell them it was closed, but instead she stood up, a genuine smile on her face.

"Hey, I thought you couldn't come in," Maple said as she reached out and commenced an unbelievably complicated handshake with the teen.

"Naw, you get my genius today," they said in a deep voice.

"Lucky me, because your genius is needed to remove all the student art and pack it up real nice for pick-up. How's that sound?"

They grunted in the affirmative.

"Tali, Anna, this is Noam. Tali and Anna both use she/her, Noam uses they/them." Maple patted them on the back before returning to her seat.

The teen grunted again, a greeting this time, and went off to do as instructed, and Tali turned to ask Anna if there was anything left on her agenda. But Anna's face had been replaced with the heart eyes emoji. "Anna?"

Her sister slowly turned toward her, as if it was difficult to peel her eyes from the other teen's back. "Hmm?"

"Uh, are we good here?" Tali shot Maple a look who seemed to also be noticing the younger woman's reaction.

"Yeah, yeah." Anna cleared her throat and closed her notebook. "It's all looking perfect."

"Why don't you go check out the student art before Noam puts it all away?"

Her sister shot out of her seat, running a recently manicured hand over her shaved head, glancing between them, and then bounding over to the other teen.

They seemed to fall into immediate conversation, though Tali wondered how much of it was grunts.

Tali and Maple stood up to start collecting all the papers they'd moved around on the table's surface.

"I mean, your sister is *cool* cool." Maple laughed. "Like I would have wanted to be her best friend in high school cool."

"Are you friends with popular kids?"

"Now? Well, I guess they are still sort of popular kids."

"Wow."

"You're surprised?"

"Well—"

"Oh my god, you thought I was a loser!"

"Not a loser. What even is a loser, though? I would have guessed you were an overly enthusiastic art kid." Tali paused for a moment, assessing Maple. "Which is what you still are."

"I'll tell you what." Maple stood, hands on hips, feet wide, in what Tali thought her therapist would call a power pose. "I was cool. If by cool you mean a hardcore goth who wrote long, pining poems for girls who didn't know they were gay yet."

"Wow, how'd you know? That's my exact definition of cool."

"Same."

"And fine, my sister *is* cool," Tali conceded. It was true. Anna had always been effortlessly kind and interesting and *interested*. Like, she wanted to know about people and listened when they talked. And never seemed to give a shit about what other people thought.

"And queer." Maple nodded her chin over to the corner where Anna was clearly, almost ostentatiously, flirting with the gallery assistant, who seemed to be communicating back entirely in facial expressions.

"What!" Tali stared open mouthed at the scene before her.

"Yeah, how do your grandparents feel about all of their grandkids being queer?" Maple went back to rolling up the plans and sliding them into their protective tubes. Casual, as if she hadn't just rocked Tali's world with her assumption.

"Why do you think we're all gay?"

"Well, I had sex with you, so you're at least a little gay." Maple winked at her, actually winked at her! Tali felt herself go a bit tomato and crossed her arms over her chest.

"I'm not talking about me, you fool." Her voice was barely above a whisper, but she poured every ounce of disapproval she had into it. "We've established I'm gay. And we did *not* have sex!"

Maple threw her head back and cackled. Then she set the tubes down and turned her full attention on Tali, taking a step closer. Tali panicked and took a step back, her ass hitting the edge of the table. She flung her hands out to stabilize herself, resting her palms on the table's surface. Maple, clearly never one to miss an opportunity to tease her, stepped forward again and rested her hands on the backs of the chairs framing Tali's body.

Tali felt herself swallow, then she heard herself swallow, realized Maple had heard it as well, and felt certain the flush on her neck could be seen from space. She also felt something else. Something far south of her throat and she immediately shoved those thoughts as far back into her mind as possible.

Tali, do not be ridiculous. You went down this road before. Remember the embarrassment of the last time. Remember this person is only fucking with you because you were such an ass. Do NOT drool, Tali!

That last internal command was the hardest to follow because there was a gorgeous butch boxing her in against a beautiful, big wooden table. A table she could lie on. A table they could—

Anna's high, melodic laughter snapped her right out of it.

She looked over to the corner where her sister stood, back turned and oblivious to her big sister's predicament. Her eyes darted back to Maple in time to catch a malicious smile curving her lips.

"Oh, Rabbi Blue, you're too easy to get all hot and bothered. And I certainly think we had sex. But if you need a refresher, I'm happy to—"

"Not here!"

Maple just blinked those bottomless brown eyes at her before seeming to come to some decision and step back, sliding her hands into her overall pockets. Disappointment boiled up in Tali faster than she could shove it back down. But she would not be investigating that. Absolutely not.

"Tali, your opinion of me." Maple just shook her head, but her voice was still light and teasing. "There are minors in the building, I would never."

"Oh my—" Tali stopped herself, forcing herself a moment to take a deep breath before trying again. "I *meant*, I don't want to *talk* about that here."

"We're excellent at communication."

"Quite."

"Quite," Maple repeated, but making it clear she was yet again mocking Tali.

Tali hmmphed and turned her attention back to the front of the gallery, but Anna and Noam were now standing out on the sidewalk, her sister leaning against a light pole watching Noam do something with the skateboard.

"You think Anna's gay?"

"Oh, I was mostly joking. Just an assumption. And you'd mentioned Beth is bi." Maple had stepped back far enough Tali felt certain the moment between them had passed. But the artist was still watching her with a look bordering between curious and hungry. Tali wondered if her own eyes gave her away like that. But gave away what? So maybe there was a little lusty tension here, fine. Just two butches interested in some sex. Or it was left over from their time together above the bar.

Nothing real.

Maple remembering Beth's name did funny things to her insides though. Warm, sweet things. Things that felt dangerously far from lust and terrifyingly near her heart.

"I mean, she's like an giant with a shaved head and a nose ring. I guess there's nothing preventing a straight teen from looking like that," Maple continued, freeing Tali of the spiraling she'd fallen into.

Maple shrugged and turned back to more tidying, but Tali hummed, watching her sister again. Anna had mentioned to her a year or two earlier she was pretty sure she was asexual, but they'd never talked about romance. How *would* their grandparents react to all three of them being queer? Most likely they wouldn't bat an eye, if history was anything to predict by.

She noticed Maple had finally finished tucking all of the tubes back onto their shelves. *Are all artists this organized? Why did I expect her to be messy?*

"So," Tali ventured, "where's this Ladino art?"

Maple's smile was blinding, set between those perfectly carved lips, below that strong nose Tali sometimes caught herself thinking about. The artist reached out and grabbed her hand, pulling her into a back room. A room full of ecstatic colors, endless looping letters, and women painted with hair like silk.

Tali squeezed the hand in hers, not wanting to let go. Wanting some way of communicating the awe she felt looking at this beautiful expression of Maple's love for her people.

Twelve — Maple

Her friends were late. They were always late. She might be the only artist she'd ever met who was chronically early. Normally she would have gone into the gallery without them, started her process of standing silently in front of each piece of work. First she liked to look. To look and try not to feel or think anything at all.

When a thought or feeling became too strong to ignore, she'd investigate it. Try to understand what it was about the piece that evoked emotion for her.

That's the way she'd been enjoying Tali recently. And holy shit did she ever enjoy Tali.

The dynamic between them had shifted ever since the visit to her studio. Maple was still flirting too much, Tali was still an eighty year-old grump in a thirty-something's body. But there was *more* now. Tali's texts—so many texts—hinted at personal facts more than not. And there was the occasional 'lol' or 'haha' to the ceaseless wave of Maple's jokes.

Before there had always come a point in the texting conversation when Tali would start to respond slower, and inevitably send something like 'we're colleagues and I'm no fun, we have to stop talking about anything not related to the project.' *Well, not that message exactly, but that was the gist of it.*

Now that never came. And Tali was often the one to initiate over these last few weeks.

There'd been a Jewish holiday Maple had never celebrated before, Shavuot. Maple admitted she wasn't sure what it was. Tali admitted she'd never known what it was until rabbinic school. Maple asked a lot of questions about why it involved cheese. There'd been a few hours of delay before she heard back from Tali around midnight. She was still up, studying with the teens.

Tali: but I'm going to leave them alone for a while

Maple: is that allowed?

Tali: weirdly, they're all actually studying

Tali: and when they're not, they're taking bets on who is more lactose intolerant

Tali: all while shoving more dairy into their mouths

Maple: aren't all Ashkenazi Jews lactose intolerant?

Tali: 1. not all my kids are Ashkenazi 2. isn't everyone lactose intolerant except like dairy cultures?

Tali: wait

Tali: are Sephardic Jews not lactose intolerant?!

Maple: idk. I don't actually like dairy. I'll ask my sister tho

Sometimes Tali had migraines and wouldn't write back for hours. And now, since their communications had become so consistent, anytime there was a multi-hour lull in conversation, Maple worried Tali was in pain.

She wished there was not a forty-five minute drive between them. Scratch that. She was incredibly grateful for the forty-five minute drive between them because who knows how spooked Tali would be if Maple showed up with ice packs and massage oil every time she didn't write back. Distance was good. It kept her from totally losing her mind over this butch.

And that was the problem. She was totally into Tali. Tali? Well, the tone of Tali's 'I hate you's' had softened. Beyond that there was a wall a foot thick.

She was so lost in thought, and in staring at her phone willing Tali to start a conversation about literally anything, that she jumped when a text finally did come in. Not from Tali. On the best friend group chat.

A picture of her, leaning against the yellow brick of the gallery building, looking absurdly forlorn.

Her head snapped up and there were her three best friends, standing together across the narrow one-way street, all with comical interpretations of her expression on their faces.

"Look who finally showed up!" She shouted and darted inside as they all started talking at once.

"So you've got it bad for this girl, huh?" Her friend Fatima knocked her elbow with her own. They were standing in front of a floor to ceiling oil painting of a field of poppies.

"You can tell because of how I'm looking at this art?"

"No, weirdo. I can tell because sixty percent of your texts recently have been about her." Fatima smirked and twirled one of her long ringlets around a finger. She was wearing a gold jumper over a black lace shirt, towering over Maple in her four inch heels. Perfect and glossy as ever. "So, is it like o*h-fish*?"

"It's nowhere near official." Maple sighed. "We're friends."

"Sex friends."

"No, like platonic friends."

"Who've had sex." Fatima raised a perfectly manicured brow in confusion.

"Well, *I* think so."

"How could that be up for debate?" Both of those brows were up, and she crossed her arms in irritation.

"You'd be surprised." Maple led them away from the painting to sit on one of the gallery's many benches. She'd never been to this gallery before, but she'd have to add it to her list of places to try to show. She loved their dedication to accessibility and their attention to detail.

"Like, did you just have a detailed sex dream about her you thought was real but it wasn't?" Fatima crossed her legs, gently nudging Maple's leg with the pointy tip of one of her heels. Clearly she was not going to let this go.

Maple looked around them to see how much privacy they had. It was a relatively empty space. She hoped for the artist's sake more people would show as the night grew later. "We're both tops."

"Like your kind of top?"

"No, but she wasn't comfortable letting a stranger fuck her."

"So, what? You two tried to out top each other all night? Was it like a staring contest?" Fatima laughed and shoved Maple's shoulder, clearly pleased with her own joke. "Wait, no! Thumb wars! Then whoever literally came out on top won?"

"You've got jokes, huh?" But Maple couldn't help but smile. She'd met Fatima on the playground in elementary school. Already Fatima had known everything she wanted out of life and Maple was drawn to her certainty. They'd remained glued at the hip all through school. When it came time for college, Maple had wanted to take a gap year and travel, but Fatima had convinced her to apply to the same art school she was going to.

It was in-between sophomore and junior years when Fatima came out as bi. Maple hadn't been surprised, but she *was* surprised when Fatima climbed into her bed one night and pressed lips to hers.

They'd tried dating for a few months, but the cracks started to show almost immediately. Maple wanted monogamy and a deep well of love. Fatima decided she wanted something more like a ship dock. To be moored to something, but not have to be present most of the year.

Their friendship hit a snag for the rest of art school, but they'd recovered eventually. Both of them wanted to move past it. Maple was pretty sure her mother had never recovered though. She loved Fatima and had been overjoyed at the idea of Jewish-Muslim grandchildren. "Double the holidays!"

Now there was a lot of love between them, but all of the friendship variety. Somewhere along the way they'd picked up Ash and Jamie and it had mellowed their friendship out. It helped that Fatima had picked up a few other adventure partners for some of her wilder ideas.

"Hello, earth to Esme." Fatima waved a hand in front of her face. "Where'd you go?"

"I was thinking about how long we've been friends. Literally three decades. Isn't that unbelievable?"

"Ew, don't reveal my age in a public place." Her best friend looked around them to make sure no potential suitors could have heard. "And why are you getting so sappy on me?"

"I'm just grateful for you."

"Wow, you've been hit by the love stick hard, huh?" Fatima narrowed her eyes at her and shook her head.

"It's a bad situation, dude," Maple admitted.

"She'll love you eventually. Who doesn't?"

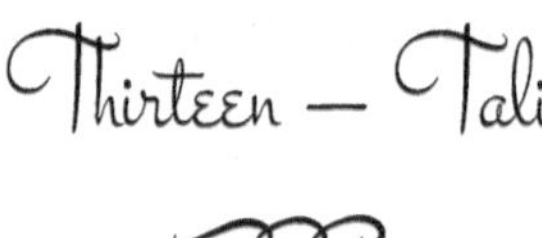

Thirteen — Tali

The air was humid and heavy in the early hours the day of the family bbq. Tali realized she'd slept with her windows open, a sheen of sweat coating her body, the sheets and blankets strewn across the edge of bed, draped onto the floor.

Like almost every morning since March, she checked her texts before anything else. As usual, there was a message from Maple. A fourth of July meme about hypocrisy and a link to an article about the history of bbqs. She opened the article to read later and gave the meme a thumbs up before rolling out of bed.

Beth was supposed to get there this morning, officially moved back to town. Glancing at the clock, she realized she might already be here.

She needed a shower, but her stomach rumbled loud enough it changed her plans. So, she made her way down the stairs, the sound of morning activity floating up to her.

Beth was leaning against the counter, holding a cup of coffee in both hands, laughing at something their grandfather was saying. She was taller than him by a few inches, though not nearly as tall as Anna, and had cropped her straight, blond hair into a chaotic bob. Her fashion sense was as tomboy chic as ever, and the only makeup she ever wore was applied as it usually was—a quick swipe of brown eyeliner and cherry chapstick.

Anna was sitting at the table, face buried in her phone, her fingers flying. Her cropped hair had grown out to delicate little brown ringlets all along her scalp. Their Bubbe was where she so often was, in the armchair they kept in the corner of the kitchen, embroidering a tongue in cheek sampler to give to one of her book club friends.

Tali felt like her heart might break in two for all of the joy flooding it as she entered the room.

The night before, buoyed by all of the passion and talent and ambition Maple was constantly showing her, she'd emailed her school advisor. Just a simple email asking how possible it was for her to maybe, one day come back and finish her last semester at rabbinical school. It'd been seven years and she was certain her advisor would have entirely written her off.

But the response came back in the same hour.

Tali,
Thank the universe you're finally writing this email. Yes, come back. We'll figure out the class load. A few requirements have changed, but we'll manage it. You might need to do a semester and a summer. Call Janet in financial aid to get all set up. Also, if you've made some Jewish educator friends in your travels, we're hiring for a few positions. Here's the link.
Can't wait to learn beside you again,
Yvette

She'd written back and let Yvette know it was just an exploratory question, but thanked her for her enthusiasm. And there was something about her advisor's certainty that the time had come, and the joy in the response, that made her feel lighter. A door she'd believed shut was actually still open all this time later.

And she'd send the job link over to Maple because one of the openings was about art. Maybe she'd know someone right for the position.

"Tali!" Beth laughed and raised her mug of coffee to her. "Are you going to stand there and watch us all morning?"

Tali walked further into the kitchen, giving her sister a hug around the taller woman's middle. "Sorry, I smell bad."

"Yeah, you do." Beth scrunched up her face, but hugged her back, careful to not spill her coffee in the process.

"Welcome home."

"I'm so excited for the BBQ today!" Her sister shouted as Tali fished oats out of the cupboard. She'd forgotten how loud her sister was. On their phone calls Tali could always adjust the volume. But she knew her grandfather appreciated Beth's ability to project, his hearing was diminishing in recent years. "And Anna tells me there's going to be a special guest."

Tali poured some water into a pot on the stove, turned the burner on, and headed to the fridge to retrieve her oat milk and almond butter and whatever berries were left from the last shopping trip. "Oh yeah? Anna, who're you texting?"

"Noam," Anna muttered, not looking up from her phone.

"Who?" Beth asked.

When Anna seemed lost back in her correspondence, Tali answered for her. "They're a teen doing some artist assistant work. We both met them like a month ago. Works with that artist we're doing—"

"Maple?" Beth interrupted, her face suddenly bright with understanding.

"How do you know who Maple is?" Tali paused while pouring her oats into the water to shoot Anna a death glare.

"Don't you have a date tomorrow?" Beth asked, ignoring her. "With someone who's not Maple?"

"Yes, she does. With a *very* nice young lady I met in potluck club," her Bubbe contributed from where she sat. "Linda. You'll love her, Tali bean. She's only a little older than you and she's a caterer."

"Lin-da," Beth mouthed dramatically at Tali with a look of wide-eyed concern. Her grandfather swatted her arm when he caught her following it with a gag-me face.

"Yes, I do." Tali bristled. "What does that have to do with Maple and what has Anna said to you?"

"Oh, I don't think you want to talk about that in the kitchen." Beth's mouth stretched into a cheshire grin.

"Beth will get to see for herself today, anyway," Anna added.

"What?" Tali turned off her burner, turning her full attention to her youngest sister. "What do you mean?"

"I invited her," Anna said, as if that was the most normal explanation in the world.

Of course she did. What a meddling matchmaker I've raised.

"Anna."

"No, you don't have time to lecture me," Anna interjected, finally meeting her gaze. "I hear that voice you're using. But we are about to start the grill. It's already noon, Tali *bean.*"

As much as she loved it when her grandmother called her that, her sisters always said it in cutesy baby voices, reminding her the name was referencing her height as the shortest in the whole family.

"And?" She turned back to mixing all her oatmeal ingredients together.

"*And*, Maple is going to be here at one, along with everyone else."

"We're going to have a chat about boundaries later," Tali hissed as she grabbed a spoon and raced back upstairs.

It was forty-five minutes later when she was done ha-cha-cha-ing down the hot oatmeal, scrubbing every inch of her body, and blow drying her short hair into something resembling a nice coif. She exited the bathroom into her bedroom, not unlocking the bathroom door into Anna's room. *Let her have to walk around as payback!* It was a holdover from childhood when Beth and Anna played pranks on each other and Tali.

She was about to whip off the towel and dive into her closet for an outfit when she realized Maple was sitting on her bed. Looking at her.

She gripped the towel tighter, conscious of how it barely met across her hips. "What are you doing in here!"

"Want me to avert my gaze?" Her tone was pure hunger, even while a teasing glint shone in her eyes.

"Why are you always early to everything? It's ridiculous! Did Anna send you up?"

"Why are you always so late? And, yes. Both of your sisters did. I'm sure they'll find this amusing that I made it just in time." She stood and took a step toward Tali, who backed up, her shoulders and ass meeting the doorframe. "You don't look embarrassed though, so maybe you're as amused."

"It's a towel, why would I be embarrassed?" She swallowed around a surprising lump in her throat. And had it suddenly gotten much warmer in the room? She glanced over to double check she'd remembered to close the windows that morning. Yep, shut tight. *The AC must be off or something.*

"What is this look then? Is it your tell?" Maple was practically purring, a sound Tali didn't realize humans were capable of until that moment.

"I'm great at poker. No tells here." But her voice was growing faint, which indeed seemed to be a tell all on its own.

"No? What about me?" Maple was almost on top of her now, and Tali was torn between putting a hand out to stop her, and gripping her floral button-up to pull her closer. So many of their conversations took place over the phone and through text. Having her there, in front of her, reminded her how handsome and tall she was. How strong her arms looked. How irritating that smirk was. "If I wanted to kiss you, for example. What would my tell be?"

"Uh." Tali felt herself at a crossroads. Maybe one they'd been at for some time. "You lick your lip."

Maple startled a little at that, the smooth top energy sliding away for a moment while she considered that information. "In a sexy way?"

And here was the moment Tali knew it was up to her to choose what path they'd take. She wasn't sure how to move forward in either direction, so she chose honesty. "Yes."

Maple's smile was staggering before it turned dangerous. She placed a hand on the wall above Tali's shoulder and leaned in until they were a whisper apart. And then she slid her tongue slowly across her bottom lip, staring into Tali's eyes.

"Yes," was all Tali could manage. *Yes, like that. Yes, please kiss me. Yes, I want this. Yes, yes, yes.*

Maple's other hand slid up the side of the towel, reaching the top and tucking her fingers under its edge. The look she gave Tali turned to one seeking permission. And Tali was going to give it, was going to enthusiastically consent to whatever came next, was going to—

"TALI!" Beth shouted as she swung the bedroom door open. "You locked the go—"

Tali moved faster than she could ever remember moving in her life. She meant to spin back into the bathroom and slam the door behind her, but Maple's hand was still tucked into the towel.

So, instead, she pulled herself free of the fabric, falling naked onto the cool blue tile. Maple, eyes round as the moon, spun away from her, holding up the towel to block the sight from Beth while she managed to move forward and shut the door with her foot.

Forget every embarrassing moment before this. This is how I die of embarrassment. There's no coming back from this. Beth will literally never let me live this down. And Maple...

Tali groaned and rolled around on the floor helplessly. She was stuck in here without her towel and with no clothing. Maybe she'd take up sewing and emerge one day in a beautiful button-up and slacks made out of the Moomins shower curtain.

Over the thumping of her heartbeat in her ears and the thick bathroom door, she could hear Beth and Maple chatting, though the words were too muffled to make out. She got up onto her knees and shuffled over to the door, pressing her ear to the crevice.

A new voice joined the other two. Maddy. Beth's childhood best friend who was always around. Over the last two years of Beth living in Atlanta, Maddy had often come over for Shabbat dinner, though she was a lapsed Mennonite. It was tradition, she was part of the family.

But why did they all have to be in her room? She groaned and slid back to the floor. She reached up and turned the doorknob, opening the door an inch.

"Is the whole world in my room?"

"Is she always this grumpy?" She heard Maple ask.

In unison Maddy and Beth said "Yes, always."

"It's pretty cute," Maple replied.

A deep warmth spread across the bridge of her nose in response to Maple's words.

"Beth, can you please bring me some clothes?"

"Wait, did I miss a nudie show?" Maddy's deep voice rang with disappointment.

"Beth!" Tali called out again in desperation.

"Yeah, yeah. Hold your horses."

When they were all safely downstairs and outside around the grill, Tali finally braved a look at Maple. The other butch sent her an immediate warm, maybe too warm, smile in response. They grabbed food from Zayde at the grill and made small talk with some of her neighbors and cousins and folks from the synagogue.

They let Anna drag them over to the garden she'd planted with all native bushes and flowers. Her own happy little bee habitat, complete with a homemade bee condo. They talked about how Maple was working on converting her truck to run on vegetable oil and how she planned to smell like fries all of the time.

Tali loved to watch Maple talk to people. It seemed so easy for her. She always knew the right tone to use, told funny little jokes to put people at ease, and expressed genuine interest in what each of them were saying.

It was all stuff Tali had to work at. The only times conversation came easily for her was when she was talking to the teens. They were so honest and straightforward, she never had to doubt where she stood with them.

When Bubbe finally made an appearance, Maple made a beeline to meet her, practically dragging Tali behind her.

"Mrs. Blue," Maple said, grin wide, hand out.

Bubbe shook her head and gently slapped her hand away. "None of that. It's Bubbe, and we hug in this family."

Maple shot Tali a quick do-*you*-hug-people look before bending and delicately wrapping her arms around the old woman's frame.

"Well, it's so good to meet you, Bubbe." Maple straightened back up and placed one of her hands on the small of Tali's back. She saw her grandmother's eyes track the movement and crinkle around the edges in happiness.

"You too, dear. Now I have to go say my hellos to the old ladies from crochet club, but you make sure Tali bean feeds you enough." She pointed a finger at Tali in a warning. They took food seriously in this family. "And Tali dear, when is Simon coming?"

"Oh, he couldn't make it. I think he's seeing someone."

"About time." Bubbe gave a sharp nod and was off to perform her reluctant hostess duties.

"How many clubs is she in?" Maple was still watching the old woman with awe in her eyes.

"I've lost count. She loves being a part of things, but she absolutely hates being the center of attention. These BBQs and parties have always been Zayde's thing." Tali nodded her chin over to where her grandfather was holding court, entertaining people from several different social circles with some unbelievable fishing story. "Let's go sit on the roof."

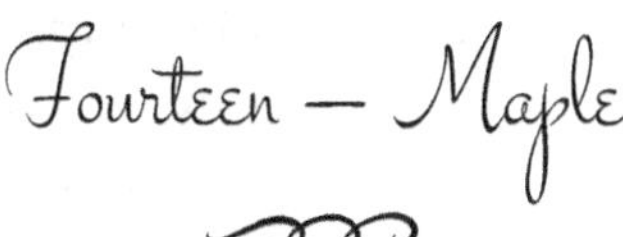

Fourteen — Maple

They snuck back upstairs with their plates stacked in desserts. Instead of going back into Tali's room, they entered the first bedroom off the landing.

"This is Anna's room now," Tali whispered. "But all three of us shared it when we were younger."

She led Maple to the window, handing her the other plate of brownies and dessert kugel so she could wrestle the glass open.

"All three of you?" Maple looked around at the modestly sized bedroom and tried to imagine them all stacked in here together. Anna had clearly redesigned it to look like an explosion of her own personality, colors and artwork covering every surface.

"Yep," Tali said as she ducked through the window out onto the roof.

Maple followed her through, handing her the plates so she could grip the windowsill and find her footing. They sat down next to each other, almost touching. "What about your room?"

"Huh?" Tali asked, half a brownie in her mouth. "Oh, it was my mom's."

"When did she pass?"

"Seven years ago. Brain hemorrhage." Tali shoved the other half of the brownie into her mouth and chewed quietly for a while. Maple didn't want to say the wrong thing, so she waited for Tali's next words. "That's why I dropped out of school."

"To help with Beth and Anna?"

"Mhmm, I'm eleven years older than Beth and she's five years older than Anna. So, we've always looked out for each other." Another silence stretched and Maple couldn't help but notice how comfortable it was, even during such a sad conversation. "I mean, we definitely still acted like sisters, but I lived at home during undergraduate to help when Anna was a baby. So, I've always been kind of her parent."

"Has it been hard?" The temptation to wrap an arm around Tali vibrated through her. She picked up a small pastry instead and started to unravel it, putting it piece by piece into her mouth.

"Yes, but the hard part is the boundary setting. She wants to act like my sister and I think of her as my kid. So, we butt heads sometimes."

"Sometimes?" Maple meant it as a tease, but Tali took it seriously.

"I mean about my dating life, and this whole college thing, and inviting you here." Tali glanced over at her, brow furrowed. "You should have talked to me before showing up."

"I guess so," Maple admitted. "I definitely was thinking of her as your sister though, and she made it sound like you were just too nervous to ask me."

"Maybe that was true." Tali's voice had grown softer, distant.

"Why are you so much older than them?"

"Uh, well, I'm adopted. My mom's best friend got pregnant when she was too young and then her parents wouldn't let her keep it. Me. Keep me. My Bubbe thought of that girl as a second daughter, so she took me in, but my mom became my mom pretty quickly. I mean, she was also just a teenager, but I was her whole world for a long time."

And then the urge was simply too much and Maple fit her hand to Tali's side, pulling her close in beside her. Tali sighed and let her head fall onto Maple's shoulder.

"And then, when I was ten she told me she was going to try to have another kid, and I was so excited to have a sibling. She used a donor. My mom was always sort of a wild child and my grandparents always supported her."

"And Anna?"

"Also a donor. The same donor. They both know their biological father, they're not interested in a bigger relationship with him, but they go see him occasionally."

"And you?"

"Hmm?" Her voice vibrated against Maple's shoulder, who was pretty sure Tali Blue was trying to covertly smell her.

"Do you see your biological people?"

"No." Her voice was a new flower bud, almost lost on the wind. "No, I did once and I won't again."

Maple squeezed her in tight, rubbing a hand slowly down her back. It felt so good to be together like this, to hold her. She thought of Fatima's reassurance and wondered if Tali was falling the way she was. She was terrified of moving too quickly in case she startled the wild animal of Tali's heart.

"What about your sisters?" Tali asked eventually as she reached for some sticky, swirly purple treat. "What are you all like together?"

"Oh man, I can't wait for you to meet them." She laughed at the mental image, particularly of how her sisters would tower over Tali as they conducted their interview.

"Mmm." The sound from Tali was the most encouraging thing she'd heard all day.

"Well, Lauren and Petra. We're all two years apart. You already know I'm the baby." Tali made the verbal equivalent of an eye roll, so Maple poked her in the side. "We fought a lot as kids. A lot. Our mother would sit us down at least once a week and have the 'family is everything' talk with us."

"How does that talk go?"

"Honestly, that's pretty much it. She would just find many different ways to say it. Sometimes she'd pepper in some stories about cousins who never made up with their siblings and how miserable their lives are now."

"Classic." Tali shifted, but, to Maple's delight, closer, so their legs pressed together.

They sat talking about family and obligation and love and everything else. Maple pulled out her notebook and made notes and even a few sketches about the way the sunset looked reflecting off the roofs around them. They sat pressed together until the darkness shooed them back into the house.

"I'll show you out," Tali said, making shy eye contact.

"Great, let me use the bathroom real quick."

"Okay, I'll meet you downstairs, gotta drop these plates in the kitchen."

Maple went into the bathroom that separated the two bedrooms, careful to lock both doors. When she came back out, she exited back into Anna's room and was surprised to find the teen there, sitting cross-legged on her bed staring at her phone screen.

"Hey, Anna."

The girl jumped several inches in the air, clearly too lost in her phone to have heard Maple's entrance.

"Oh, wow, hi." She clutched her phone to her chest and took a deep breath. "Sorry, wow, that was terrifying."

"Didn't mean to scare you!" Maple laughed. "I was just about to head out. Thanks for inviting me. This was so fun."

"Mmmhmmm." Anna stretched the sound to its breaking point. "You two were missing for most of it."

"Oh, just some roof time." She waved a hand at the still open window and rubbed the other down her neck, conscious of what Tali had been saying about wanting clearer boundaries with Anna.

"An old school Tali Blue move," Anna said knowingly. "But, uh, did she tell you she has a date tomorrow?"

That was like a bucket of ice. They certainly weren't dating, but they also weren't *not* dating. *I wouldn't go on a date with someone else right now.*

"Like a whole evening. Dinner, movie, probably drinks. You should tell her not to go," Anna added before returning her attention to her phone.

Maple made her way downstairs, found Tali in a heated debate about how quickly egg salad needed to be refrigerated with Beth and Beth's maybe girlfriend, or had they said they were just friends? It didn't matter. She wanted to get into her truck and spend some alone time with her feelings.

"Maple!" The warmth and ease in Tali's voice only made it worse. *We are terrible at communication. Still.*

"Hey," she said, trying to sound at least half as happy as Tali did. "It was so great to meet you all. Please tell Bubbe she hosted a fabulous party."

Beth laughed, turning to make some inside joke about the word fabulous with her not-girlfriend. Tali raised an eyebrow at Maple, starting to move toward her.

"I'll see you later, Tal." And she left.

The next day she distracted herself with as much admin work as she could shove into the daylight hours. She knew she should tell Tali how she was feeling, but she was still terrified of the return of the morning-after Tali. That cold, abrupt creature that could go from a night of connection to ten yards of emotional distance without blinking.

She also applied to one of the jobs Tali had sent her way. The rabbinic college was hiring an art teacher for a semester-long test. She loved teaching kids, but the idea of being able to combine her Jewish identity and her career, the way she had been with her Ladino project, felt so right.

When night came though, Maple let herself type before thinking better of it.

> Maple: So, how was your date?

> Tali: how do you know I was on a date?

The reply was immediate and Maple could imagine the suspicious narrowing of Tali's eyes as she typed. She felt a smile pull at her lips despite herself. Not wanting to out Anna, she fibbed.

> Maple: Oh... my assistant

> Tali: you speak grunts now?

> Maple: Not no

> Tali: Hmmphmm

When nothing else came after a minute, Maple wrote back.

> Maple: Uh what?

> Tali: That was me grunting my date answer to you. What? The wrong dialect?

Maple laughed into her silent apartment.

Oh, so she's funny now, huh?

> Maple: Must be - you'll have to use English
> for me

> Tali: Or Ladino

> Maple: Have you been studying up?

> Tali: you wish.

> Maple: yeah, I do

A long pause now. Probably she'd put her phone down, annoyed with Maple's constant flirtation. She kicked herself mentally. But then again, texts could be interpreted in endless ways. Maybe she'd just been interrupted. Maybe she suddenly fell asleep because the date had been so exhausting. Maybe she was at her date's house right now.

No, no. Better to not start imagining that option.

Then the three little dots started dancing across the screen and all hope was restored. Until they stopped again and Maple cursed the invention of cell phones.

Then it rang.

"H-hello?" Maple answered, fumbling the phone in her eagerness.

"I'm tired of typing."

"Likely story, you just missed my voice."

"It was fine. The date," Tali said, entirely ignoring Maple's comment.

"Oh wow, don't go over-describing it now. You know I hate details."

"I hate you."

"So you love to tell me. But let's see, it's like, uh..." She pulled away from the phone to look at the time. "Wow, it's barely eight pm and you're texting, now calling, me. So it can't have gone well."

"Maybe it was a super cute lunch date."

Maple took a quick shot of her own skeptical face, an eyebrow raised and the corner of her mouth quirked up and sent it back in response.

"You are ridiculous. Did you *text me* a photo while we're on the phone?"

"I might be ridiculous, but I'm also extremely cute." Maple waited for Tali's snort and was rewarded by a particularly disbelieving one. "*And* I'm well informed. I know it was supposed to be dinner and a movie. Classic stuff there."

"Yeah, well informed by *Anna*. Don't try to protect her. A long talk is in store for that girl. And, if you must know, we didn't make it to the movie."

A sentence Maple would have stressed over if they were still texting. Could mean dinner had been so great they'd shot right back to the car and fucked hard enough to throw the car into drive and cause a crash.

What is wrong with you?

But Tali's tone said it all.

"Oof, that good huh?"

"What can I say? You've ruined me."

Maple had expected another goofy joke or two. The best she had expected was they'd tease each other for a while. A few more minutes on the phone, maybe an hour or two of lazy texting.

Normal, casual friend stuff that normal, casual friends who were definitely not sexually interested in each other did.

And then say their good nights and continue the slow, steady trek toward real friendship. She certainly, even in her wildest imagination, hadn't expected Tali would actually start flirting back. Not really. But maybe she wasn't, maybe this was just a meaner joke. *She's not great at jokes.*

"What's that now?"

"A little honesty. A little bravery. You know, that stuff you're always yammering on about."

Maple chose to ignore that dig in favor of falling hopelessly into, well, hope.

Ruined her? For what?

"How?" Maple cleared her throat when her voice came out far too close to a squeak.

"What?"

"How did I 'ruin' you?"

"Listen, Linda was perfectly nice."

"Linda is the date?" She didn't want to know, she wanted to know everything. She wanted this to last forever.

"Yeah, Linda was the date. And she seemed great. Exactly the kind of woman I've gone for in the past." Tali's own voice was too measured. What Maple wouldn't give in that moment for a teleportation device.

"Aaand?"

"And, well, honestly I sat there thinking about how objectively beautiful she was."

"Nice." She kept her voice as flat as she could.

"It was. But also that's it. I knew she was beautiful, but I didn't feel it. Not like when I look at you." Maple could hear Tali take in a steadying breath. Heard the rustling of Tali's sexy, soft body adjusting in blankets. "I feel how handsome you are in my bones. I think about your strong hands on my arms, the way you grabbed me on that first night. The way your binder peeks out. The way your lips look wrapped around my fingers. I feel it like an ache. I *want* to hurt like that."

Maple was certain all of the oxygen in the world was gone in response. At least all the air in her studio and apartment. And suddenly it was so hot in her room. She glanced up to make sure the fan was still on and then back at her phone and felt hot all over again.

Be cool, bitch. You're a smooth, toppy motherfucker. And with that internal pep talk, her super smooth butch mouth said the words, "Oh, thanks."

WHAT THE FUCK, DUDE? Betrayed by my own mouth.

"Ha! 'Thanks.' *Months* of flirting *at* me and I finally flirt back and I just get some gratitude?"

"Well, isn't gratitude like—" She trailed off, having literally no idea where she'd planned to take that sentence.

"Okay, cool, that's cool. I'm going to—"

"You called me your 'good girl,'" Maple blurted out in an attempt to keep this conversation going.

"What?"

"When we were fooling around," Maple clarified. "You called me that and it was the first time anyone ever had and I liked it."

"Oh."

"Do you also like to be called that?"

"Oh, wow, no." Tali's laugh came through the phone so sweetly. It was the least guarded she'd ever heard her be. It was mesmerizing.

"What words do you like?"

"What're we doing, Maple?" The words were exactly what Maple would expect from her, but they lacked their typical suspicious edge.

"Whatever you want, Tali."

"I want you to top me."

"I'll get in my truck right now." Maple stood as she spoke. Ready to blow every yellow light on the drive.

"No." Tali laughed again and Maple wanted to paint it. She needed some way to bottle it and be able to turn it over and look at it from every angle. It was such a gift. "It'll take too long, and I'm not having sex in my grandparents' house."

"How long has it been?" Maple settled back onto her bed reluctantly, still feeling the urge to drive, to be closer.

"Oh, too, too long," Tali groaned. "Until you."

"I thought that wasn't sex."

"I hate you," Tali said again in a voice that sounded exactly the opposite. "It was. And it was good."

"Yes, it was." Maple took a deep breath attempting to calm the fluttering in her stomach. "How do you want me to top you now, Tali? You want to video call me?"

"No! That's too much. Just tell me how good it will feel to have you inside of me."

"Topping from the bottom already." Maple slid herself free of her boxers. "Tali, I'm going to make you feel so good you'll finally tell me all those feelings you keep wrapped up so tight."

"Show me yours, Esme Pull."

"I've already done that."

"You tease too much, just fuck me." Tali's voice was that impatient growl Maple hadn't heard since the night they spent together. It felt like torture to be so far from her.

"Bossy,." But they both knew Maple liked it.

And so they spent the next hour pushing each other. Maple described each way she planned to make Tali scream her name, how she'd make her glad to bottom. How she'd fuck her until there was nothing but two bodies panting in the dark. She wanted to mark her, exhaust her, worship her.

She wanted to make Tali love her.

"This is where I'd cuddle you."

"This is where I'd consider letting you."

"Aftercare is important," Maple said in her best teacher voice.

"Mmm."

"Oh, another grunt. Using my superior translation skills I

see this one means 'oh definitely, cuddling sounds great, thanks.'"

"Sure, that, and I get super sleepy after orgasms." Tali's voice was thick and slow, a soft landing after so many hard, hot words.

"Good to know. Next time I'll be prepared to tuck you in as you come down."

"So, I might fall asleep. Don't freak and think I smashed and dashed."

"What a classy butch you are. Well, before you pass out from my superior lovemaking—" Maple imagined the endless eye roll she'd earn in response to that line and snorted, "I have a question for you."

"Gross. And sure, what's up?"

"I have an art show tomorrow at my studio. I'm showing my Ladino project so far."

"Oh, cool."

"So, yeah, I was wondering if you could come?" As soon as she said it she decided to follow Tali's lead and be brave. "And be my date?"

The brief silence was too much. *Maybe she's asleep. Or maybe she's shutting down yet again. Why is she like—*

"I'd love to."

Maple fist-pumped into the air before promising to send a follow-up text with the details. When they hung up she giggled like a child into her pillow for longer than she'd ever admit to anyone.

Fifteen — Tali

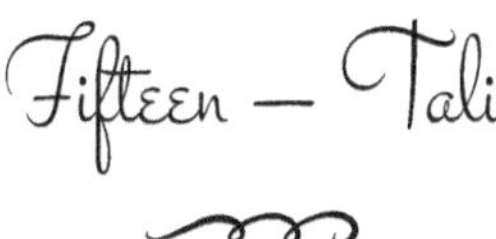

"You could have brought Anna. She could have hung out with my squad while you and I have some alone time." Maple actually raised her eyebrows suggestively. Tali summoned every ounce of willpower she had to not roll her eyes.

The art show was packed. Tali knew Maple was talented and beloved, but clearly hadn't understood how widely known she was too.

"So, where are Fatima and Company anyway?"

"Ha, they're mingling. Probably all together, but mingling. Funny, you remember my rude nickname." Maple took another micro step closer. Tali did her best to squash the response thrill. They'd snuck off to the least populated corner, farthest from the food table. Tali was back in what was becoming her favorite position, against the wall, watching Maple descend upon her.

She'd have to talk to her therapist about what that was doing to her identity as a top. *Oh, Carol. Maybe I should find a queer therapist so she can stop sweating every time I enter her office and start talking about dykenamics.*

"Honestly it seemed right. You talk about Fatima and her

wild adventures all the time, and your other two friends seem so—"

"Boring?"

"Wow, no. Settled!" Tali laughed. "You think your best friends are boring?"

"*I* don't, but they're my friends! And settled is a good word. They are. Settled. Jamie and Ash have always found ways to be happy with whatever life brings them. It's impressive."

Maple kept talking, starting another wild Fatima story about her tri-continental search for the perfect shade of blue. Tali was only half listening, suddenly caught up on the idea of being happy with whatever life offers.

The rest of the night was a blur of introductions Tali would never remember, hors d'oeuvres that had to be eaten, and smiling so hard her cheeks hurt. She was out of practice and way out of her comfort zone. Her hand kept finding Maple's, the other butch's strong fingers threading through her own and tugging her closer. When Maple hesitated before handing her a cracker stacked with what looked like cheese and then ate it herself, declaring she was saving Tali from the wretched taste of drizzled honey, well, Tali thought about the word *swoon*.

Fatima kept stealing her away to gush over Maple's art between rounds of intrusive questions. Tali loved it. It had been a long time since she'd spent any real time with people other than her sisters or the teens at work. It occurred to her how lonely she'd been without friends the last several years.

"I'm so glad Esme finally has someone to talk about all

that save the earth stuff she's always on about." Fatima rolled her eyes but shot Tali a smile that made it clear she was joking.

"Do most people call her Esme?" Tali knew they'd dated before, but had a hard time picturing it. It was definitely before Maple had come out as butch for butch. Fatima was a femme goddess with shining black curls down her back and a perfect face of sultry makeup. Her long acrylics came to sharp points and delicate gold chain bracelets slid along her toned arms.

"Just me and her mother." Fatima's face pulled into a mischievous expression. "Even her sisters call her Maple, but I like having a fun best friend nickname and I think it annoys her only a little bit."

"I'm glad she has someone in her life who's purposefully annoying *her*."

"Oh, you act like you don't love it when she teases you, but I just met you, Tali, and even I can see how much you like it."

"Can we go back to talking about the environment now?" Tali grumbled, only slightly embarrassed. Secretly, she was pleased Maple's best friend seemed to enjoy her.

"I suppose. Don't want to scare you off. Yes, Maple loves to get on a soapbox about the earth, while she's still living this bougie life here. *That's* my favorite topic, in the whole green scheme, is how deep capitalism has its claws into environmentalism. It makes people think the only way to be eco-friendly is to be rich."

They had just made it back to the group and Maple caught the end of their conversation. "Oh, light topics for the first meeting, huh?"

"Darling, you know I don't do chitchat." Fatima waved a hand in front of her as if to disperse the very idea of such a thing.

Each time Tali was returned to Maple, she wrapped her

hand around the tall artist's bicep and laughed at whatever joke she was telling. Her fingers pressed there as if they had a right to be there. As if they were way past being two ill-fitting colleagues who drove each other to their wits' ends. Like they were now people who touched each other casually, easily. It was thrilling. It was terrifying.

That's not who we are.

Or if it was, Tali realized she hadn't been paying any attention.

Eventually the night died down and people said their goodbyes. She stayed tucked into Maple's side, a brave hand venturing into one of her back pockets, waving at all of the people whose names she'd already forgotten.

They grabbed the trays of food and brought them back to the tiny closet that served as the gallery's staff kitchen. The staff being Maple and Noam, there was never a need for much more space. They worked in relative silence, moving around one another to pack away leftovers and cork half empty bottles of wine.

The closer to finished they got, the more Tali became aware of a static in the room, a thickness made of tiredness and lust and proximity.

She turned to see if Maple felt it too, only to find the butch leaning against the single counter space, watching her.

"Am I doing all the work while you supervise?" Tali tried to look irritated, but she would have happily done that for her, to celebrate the progress of the art and thank her. Thank her for what, Tali wasn't ready to examine, but she knew she was grateful.

"Just at the end here," Maple said, voice low and heavy as the air around them. "Your ass was too distracting to look away from."

"Oh, is that right?" Tali knew her face was coloring, she hoped the room was dark enough to hide it. She was so unused to being the object of desire, of being watched in that way. It felt like a bruise. Like touching a soft spot she'd forgotten about.

Maple stepped forward, a shadow slanting across her face. "Yes, Tali. I think about your body often."

"Oh." Tali's breath came out shaky. Every handhold, every touch of the artist's muscled arms, every time Maple had slid her fingertips along Tali's lower back that night vibrated through her. She thought back to their phone sex the night before and realized how much easier that had been for her. How she could hide behind the distance, disguised in her own voice.

This felt raw. And she wanted all of it.

"Do you still want me to top you, Tali?" Maple still stood in shadow, her hands tucked into her pockets, looking entirely at ease. Tali was sure she looked panicked, regardless of her desire.

"Yes," she managed.

"Yes, what?"

"Yes, please."

"Turn around, Tali, and put your hands on the wall."

No sooner had she complied than Maple was pressed against her, hands firm at her hips, pulled her ass against herself.

"Where can I touch you?" Maple whispered in her ear.

"Everywhere." It was too much, the admitting of it. The exposed need in her voice. She closed her eyes and took a steadying breath. "I trust you, Maple."

"Fuck, Tali." Maple leaned in and took the skin where neck met shoulder between her teeth and gently bit.

Tali kept her hands glued to the wall, determined, for once in her life, to take what she wanted. And what she wanted was to do as she was told. To be obedient to this woman until the edges between them blurred.

Maple's hands worked Tali's shirt free of her pants, quickly ran up the front, unbuttoning every last button. Then she took her time running them slowly over Tali's binder, spiraling around her hard nipples. All the while continuing to alternate between biting and licking the sensitive skin of Tali's neck.

She was in a frenzy. They'd only started and already the sensations washed over Tali in waves. She shivered as Maple worked her binder up enough to uncover her nipples and pull them between strong fingers.

"I want you," she moaned, her voice foreign to her ears.

"You have me," Maple said against her skin.

She panted and whined as Maple unbuttoned her pants, sliding them and the boxers below to her knees. She spread her feet as wide as she could take them and mentally willed Maple to just fuck her already. But she wouldn't ask because the exquisite torture of waiting was too good.

"Do you want me to fuck you?" Maple asked in a voice so steady and firm Tali almost whimpered. "Do you want me to make you come right here?"

"Yes, please, please." Tali thought she might cry. Standing there bracketed by the wall and this tall, gorgeous butch, lewdly half-undressed, she felt safer than she had in a long time.

Maple moved the faintest tips of her fingers up and down Tali's thighs until they trembled. "Will you scream my name when you come, Tali?"

"Fuck, I'll scream anything you want when I come."

"I love seeing you like this," Maple said as she circled closer to Tali's center.

"Desperate?"

"No. All mine." She put a hand on Tali's shoulder, bending her forward.

She finally moved those teasing fingers to her soaking wet folds and Tali had to fight to not let her knees buckle. Maple eased along each lip, gently tugging on them and kneading them with her knuckles. Tali bucked back against her, but the hand on her upper back steadied her.

Maple slipped through her slit, lingering in unhurried circles around her aching clit. Tali bit her lip to keep from any further begging, but she doubted she could last much longer.

Finally, Maple dove into her, moaning while she pressed two fingers in to the last knuckle. Tali gasped, her core throbbing in response. She pushed back as much as Maple would allow her and ground into those fingers.

So many nights she'd imagined those clever hands on her, inside of her, and nothing compared to the real fullness of them.

Maple began to thrust, pushing her own pelvis against the hand between them. Tali gasped with each new entrance, her pussy dripping down her thighs.

The hand on her back moved to grab one of Tali's hands. "Can you hold yourself up with one?" Maple's voice wasn't steady anymore. It was hoarse and tight, as if she too was on the verge of collapse.

Tali only managed to nod, the relentless thrusting making it impossible to string sounds together. Maple saw her assent and moved Tali's left hand behind her, placing it on her own ass. "Hold yourself open for me, Tali."

She did as she was told, feeling much more naked than before. Aware of Maple seeing so much of her. *I want her inside of me everyday.* The thought came unbidden but she couldn't examine it now, as a new sensation rocked her mind. Maple had pulled out of Tali, only to push slowly back in with two fingers in her pussy and a knuckle pressing against her ass.

Her breath hitched and she started to squirm, but whether it was to get closer or farther from the new sensation, she couldn't tell. All she knew for sure was that Maple was back to pushing her hips against that hand and her clit was jumping at the heady feeling.

Maple's free hand reached under Tali, running along her jaw until she reached her mouth. Tali took those clever fingers in, sucking them, stroking them with her tongue. She heard the woman topping her moan as Tali took them into her throat. After fucking Tali's mouth with them for a minute, Maple pulled them free. She slid them down Tali's body to catch a nipple and tug in time with the motion of her hips.

"Please. It's too much."

"Are you ready to come for me?" Voice like hot syrup in the dark.

"Yes, please, I need—"

But Maple had already released her nipple to apply the same attention to her swollen clit. Tali felt her eyes roll back at the sheer height of need she'd reached.

"Come for me, Tali," Maple demanded as she rubbed the very head of her clit, still sliding those fingers in and out of her, bringing her to the brink with each motion. "Come for me, now."

And Tali came, hard and long, shuddering around Maple's fingers. She came not so much shouting Maple's name as gasping it, drinking it in, bathing in the sensation of it on her tongue. Her whole body shook and her mind just played on loop.

Maple, Maple, Maple, Maple

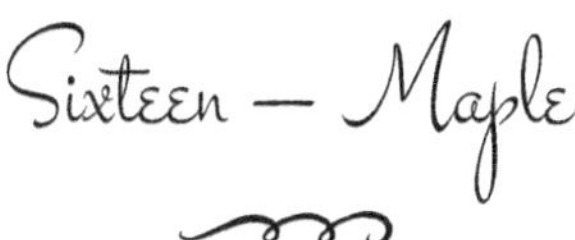

Sixteen — Maple

Maple slowly slid herself out of Tali, the woman letting out a hiss at the overwhelm of sensation. She ran one hand down Tali's back, soothing her.

When Tali managed to stand, Maple turned to wash her hands. By the time she was done, Tali had her pants back up and her binder pulled down. "What can I do for you?"

Her voice was already so sleepy, so sweet. Her eyelids were heavy and the look of pure bliss across her face made Maple want to drag her to the studio and sketch her before fucking her again on top of the canvas.

Self-control, Maple. It's late, put her to bed.

"I'm good, sweetheart." Maple paused. She hadn't meant to use any sort of honey sweet name with Tali, at least not out loud. But she didn't seem to notice. "Let's get you to bed."

"I need some air." Tali gulped, fanning herself. "Can we step outside for a second?"

"Sure, of course." Maple led her out the side door, holding the door open for her. Tali leaned against the brick, spreading her arms wide and closing her eyes. "You okay?"

They stood on the street of the cute little town Maple had

picked because it was the right mix of nowhere and some-where. She could hear the sound of men laughing, the thump of dance music behind them. But all she could see was Tali.

"Hmm?" Tali asked without opening her eyes. "Oh, yeah. I'm perfect. You fucked all the emotions loose. Gotta get some air in there to sort them. Ya know?"

She didn't know, but she wanted to. She wanted to know everything about her. She stepped forward and traced her fingers along Tali's cheek. She turned toward the touch and kissed the very tip of Maple's pointer finger.

"Tali," Maple started, she was going to say so many things about feelings and she was going to do it right now before they simply burst from her chest.

A car roared to life down the road, some asshole with his overcompensation noise machine. It grew louder as it reached them, both of them turning to glare at its approach.

The vehicle slowed as it moved past, a furious voice shouting out obscenities about their masculine appearances at them before peeling away.

They stood frozen for a moment, Maple's hands still on Tali's hips, both of them watching the empty street. It felt unbelievable that they'd gone from pure bliss to utter bullshit in such a short window.

"I gotta go." Tali pushed away from the wall and left Maple's side.

"What?" Maple's body clenched in disbelief. "Because of that?"

"No." But Tali continued toward her car.

"What the fuck, Tali?" Maple started after her. "If anyone should be upset, it's me."

Tali swung back toward her, a look of concern across her face. "You're right. Are you going to be okay? Do you want to call your sisters to come?"

"My sisters?" Maple stopped a few feet from her. "Why are

you leaving? Who the fuck cares what some asshole thinks about us?"

"It's not that—"

"You're right it's not about that." Maple could feel anger reaching its long fingers up her throat. She hated being angry, it made her feel sick. But she had a right to be angry! She wasn't going to lose...whatever this was becoming because of *a man*. Absolutely not. "I thought we'd moved past this."

"We?" Tali's voice shifted from worried to stiff, stern, bordering on icy. "Who is we? We the United States? 'Cause no, *we* have not moved past homophobia. *We* haven't moved past misogyny, or maybe he was attempting some transphobia."

"That's not what I meant." Maple wanted to get them both walking back to the building. She wanted to have this argument up in her apartment where they'd sort out all their issues and end it with some more sweet, sweet sex.

"Okay. If you meant *we* as in *us*," Tali waved an agitated hand between their bodies. "Then there's not much of a *we* there, is there?"

"Tali, that's so not—"

"No, don't say my name like you know me. We're not pals. And anything we've done otherwise was a mistake."

"Oh, here we go." Maple rolled her eyes and shoved her hands into her pants pockets. "I *knew* you were going to try to pull this shit. Oh, what? Are we *colleagues*? Yeah, that makes a whole lot of sense, Tali. That's definitely how we've been talking to each other for almost *six months*. You must be the slowest moving lesbian on the face of the earth. Six months of this with anybody else and I'd be married at this point."

Tali's mouth dropped open and Maple could hear how those words must have sounded to someone as tightly wound as Tali, but she didn't care. She wanted to be a messy butch and claim they'd just been coworkers this whole time? Fine,

Maple could be messy too. And she was done being careful with Tali Blue. It was time she came to her senses and realized Maple was a goddamn catch.

However, when Tali snapped her mouth shut, turned on her heel, and strode back to her own car, quite a bit of her confidence evaporated.

"Where are you going?"

"Home," Tali called over her shoulder, not bothering to turn around.

"*Home?* It's the middle of the night. You're going to drive for an hour right now? Tali, come on. Let's go up to my place and we can figure this out there."

Tali froze in place for a minute. When she spun to face Maple her face was a mask of cold indifference.

"Maple, that was never an option. I was always going home. We're not in a relationship, despite the wedding bells playing in your head."

"Oh yeah, that's what's happening. I just *love* what a prickly *little* cactus you are and have been doodling on the back of my canvases 'Mrs. Esme Blue.'"

"Stop making fun of how short I am, it's annoying. Who cares that I'm short, *Maple*." Maple bit back a smile at how cute, and yes, short, Tali looked in that moment as she hunched her shoulders up indignantly. "All of this is too much for right now."

"This might be the stupidest fight two people have ever had." Maple had felt the air go out of the argument. She watched Tali deflate as she seemed to realize the same thing, a small smile tugging at the corners of her mouth.

"Alright, yeah, maybe." Tali turned to get into her car. Just before sliding in, she said over her shoulder, "I'll call you tomorrow and apologize. For this fight and for not going home with you and letting you fuck me silly a second time."

"Yeah, that is a shame."

"Space though—"

"Makes the heart grow fonder," Maple offered.

"Right." And with that, Tali was gone.

Her empty, dark apartment greeted her and she felt a well of sadness uncover deep in her stomach.

She texted her friend group. Unsurprisingly, only Fatima was up and she called her right away.

"Hey babe." Fatima's voice trilled through the speaker. "What's going on?"

"Tali and I got into a fight." She sounded so small to her own ears.

"About who loves who more?" Fatima sounded genuinely confused, which was reassuring in a way. "I don't understand, when I left both of you were all moony with each other."

"We had sex."

"Well, good for you. Was it bad? Is that why you fought?" The hiss of embarrassment on her behalf made Maple laugh.

"No, it was..." She paused, searching for a word big enough. "It was everything. She let me top her and I made her come until she cried in my studio kitchen."

"Holy shit." Fatima's tone had shifted to impressed. "I thought the problem was you were both tops?"

"She's more of a switchy top? Or just a top and labels are complicated? And, before you say some shit again, I don't want to top her *because* she's a top. I want to top her because I want to give her everything and take everything in return."

"That's sort of romantic, dude."

"Thanks. I try."

"So the fight was after?"

"Yeah, some douchebag yelled some bigoted shit when we were taking a little break outside and she totally shut down." Maple ran a hand over her face, regretting not yelling back. But that was her firm policy: don't feed the trolls.

"Are you okay?" Fatima sounded ready to go hunt the guy down herself.

"Yes, yes. And it was so fast." Maple stopped, replaying the moment when she saw Tali's eyes shutter. "It can't be why she left."

"And what about you?" Fatima asked, clearly prodding at something Maple wasn't looking at.

"What?"

"What is this reaction about? Because as much as I'm always here for your big butch feelings, you wouldn't normally call me about this in the middle of the night."

"I deserve someone who wants me." A tiny tendril of the anger from earlier unfurled in her chest.

"Yes, you do," Fatima agreed. "But also, sometimes you do this."

"Do what?"

"Your pride can be so easily bruised, babe." Fatima was the softest Maple had ever heard her be. "Not everyone is trying to disrespect you when they pull away. Sometimes people are just hurting."

Her best friend was right. The tightness in her chest hadn't dissipated when the fight had ended. Sure, they still needed to make up. Preferably in some way that involved very few clothes and a lot of honesty. But there was something harder behind all of that.

"I think I'm letting Tali be a symbol sometimes." She spoke slowly, her brain pulling together the strings in the moment. "Like, she's my clearest connection to the Jewish world right now. She's basically a rabbi. I think I'm letting my baggage about all of my history, all the rejection, pool up around this relationship."

"Yeah," was all Fatima said, but Maple could almost hear her nodding sympathetically.

"I'm afraid she doesn't see me." Tears threatened, drowning the tendril of anger.

"And maybe you're also afraid she does?"

She sighed into the dark of her apartment, wishing that moving through something was as easy as acknowledging it. "I'll talk to her."

Seventeen — Tali

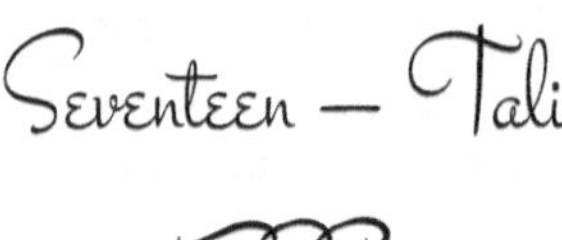

"There's another bad review." Simon was sitting at the front of the classroom, head in his hands. He quietly whispered the bad news to Tali who tried to make her hums sound as sympathetic as possible.

"How long has he been like this?" Tali asked at full volume to the room full of teens who were all paying absolutely no attention to her or Simon.

Jonah, her favorite student—which, of course, she'd never admit—turned toward her voice and shrugged.

"Been like what?" Cassie, the youngest teen of the group, asked from the back of the room.

Bless these teenagers for their inattentive natures.

"Okay, Si, let's get you back to your office," Tali said quietly, patting Simon on the shoulder. Raising her voice, she addressed the room again. "Hey, team? It's the end of summer. Today's a free day and if your parents ask, we talked about preparing for school life. I'll be back in five minutes and I *will* ask the class snitch if anyone did anything illegal."

A few kids cheered, and teased each other about who she

might be calling a snitch, and mostly they all continued doing whatever they'd been doing before.

I love them.

When she and Simon got back to his office, she shut the door behind them.

"What on earth is wrong with—" she started before realizing he was crying. Big, heavy tears streaming down his face to hit his stubble and make it glisten in the fluorescent lights. "Simon? What is going on? You're not crying about this cookie thing are you?"

"What?" Simon let out a little hiccuping cry. "Oh, no. Tali, you must think I'm a clown."

"Only on occasion."

He let out a sad little laugh at that before slumping into his office chair and reaching for a tissue.

"No, I just, oh, it's so stupid."

"Simon, whatever it is, it's not stupid," Tali reassured him. She'd never seen him be anything but the utmost professional. And she was all for crying at work, it was human, healthy. But to have turned into a zombie in front of the teens? *Bizarre.* "Tell me, get it off your chest."

"Well, I've been seeing someone," Simon started slowly, dabbing at his eyes.

"Yeah, I'd guessed. There's a little bet going around the admin office about who it is." She realized her mistake and added, "but obviously I didn't tell you that."

"That's just great." A few more tears welled up. "Well, you can tell them all it doesn't matter because it's probably over. Which feels unbelievable because I was thinking about proposing."

"What!" Tali couldn't stop herself. "How long have you been seeing this person?"

"Since April" He hiccuped.

Shorter than I've known Maple. Maybe she's right, I do move slowly.

"So, what happened?" She handed him another tissue when the one he'd been using started to disintegrate.

"I said a stupid thing." His voice shook dangerously and she wished she knew how to comfort people in any real way.

"Tell me," Tali prodded. "I say stupid stuff all the time."

"She's Mrs. McCutcheon's granddaughter."

"Who?" Tali wondered if she was supposed to have remembered that name.

"Mrs. McCutcheon. You know, from the bakery."

And suddenly all the pieces clicked into place. "The dusty, bad cookie bakery?"

Simon nodded pitifully.

"You told her that her grandmother's cookies are terrible?"

He nodded again, his facial features seeming to all slump.

"Oh, Simon." Tali bit her lip searching for a sympathetic thing to say. "You're right, that definitely wasn't a great move. But I'm sure you can patch things up. You said it yourself, you loved those cookies. Just blame it all on me, or on the anonymous commenter."

He tried a few different sounds, but none resulted in words, until he finally let his head drop to the desk while he cried.

"I have to get back to those kids, Si," Tali said, an equal mixture of relief and regret in her voice. "But I'm going to ask Gina to come sit with you for a while, okay?"

Gina was their octogenarian cantor who led all the songs for the services. She was the most comforting person Tali knew.

Simon flopped his head around in what she decided to take as a nod.

Later that afternoon, after she drove Simon home and promised him that he'd think of something to make things right, she turned to her own mistakes.

She was embarrassed by her behavior the night before. And she wanted to kick herself for ruining the comedown of the best sex of her life. Well, letting some random stranger ruin it, but still.

She sat in her car outside her grandparents' home and took a deep breath before calling Maple.

"Oh, hello," Maple said brightly. "How's it going?"

"You don't sound mad at me," Tali said, feeling her brows come together in suspicion.

"I'm not," Maple laughed. "Am I supposed to be?"

"Did I dream up last night?" Tali was startled, this was nowhere near how she'd imagined this conversation would go.

"I don't know," Maple said, her voice dropping to a flirtatious tone. "Did we have the same dream? Mine involved me bending you over getting a good feel for how wet—"

"Okay! Okay, stop it." Tali rolled her eyes. Of course she was flirting while Tali was trying to apologize. "I'm calling to say I'm sorry—"

"For not staying and letting me explore that ass some more?"

Her face was instantly the surface of the sun. This woman was a menace. "For not staying and talking it out with you, Maple."

"Tomato, tomato," Maple joked. "Okay, but I'm being serious now. Tell me."

Tali met her own gaze in the rearview mirror and gave

herself a micro pep talk. *Be a badass, Tali. Badasses talk about their feelings.* "I panicked, and it wasn't about that jerk."

"Okay, what was it about?"

"The people in my life right now, they've been in my life forever." Tali let out a breath she didn't realize she'd been holding. It was easier to be open once you opened the door a crack. "And, well, I had a good therapy session this morning—"

"Did you give my hellos to Carol?" Maple interjected.

"And I realized," Tali said a little louder, ignoring Maple. Though remembering her therapist's name was probably a relationship milestone. "That while you might think we're moving slowly, this is pretty fast for me. When my mom died, I cut off the life I'd been living and my circle shrank. By a lot."

"That makes sense." Maple's voice was careful and soft now.

"And I haven't let anyone new in." Tali heard the hitch in her own voice and took a few deep breaths. "I want to let you in. I need to figure out how to do that."

"Thank you. It means a lot that you're telling me this."

"Well, thank you for listening to it," Tali replied, her face heating again. *See, you can do feelings!* "How are you, really?"

"Well, I also had a revelation," Maple said. "With therapist Fatima. Actually, two revelations."

"Wow. Is Fatima licensed?"

"That's one of the realizations. I've decided to go back to therapy." Maple sounded genuinely enthused at the idea. "Which is related to the other piece, the part that more directly concerns you."

"Oh?" She fought the feeling of panic. Maybe they should have shared in the reverse order? What if she had been so vulnerable just to get broken up with right now? And could you be broken up with if you'd never agreed you were dating?

"All that rejection stuff, the racism and Ashkenormativity

from all the times I've tried to be involved in mainstream Jewish stuff before?"

She said it like a question, so Tali said, "I remember."

"I'm letting it get all tangled up in us. And I want to work on processing all that and doing some healing and not let it poison all this goodness we have."

"Oh." The relief washed over her. *Not being dumped.* "I think that's a great decision. To go to therapy for that."

"And Tali?" The teasing tone was clearly on its way back in and Tali braced herself.

"What?" She asked, sighing.

"I look forward to you *letting me in* over and over and over." Maple laughed and Tali felt around for her irritation, but, alarmingly, only found amusement.

Still, she said, "you're so fucking annoying."

Eighteen — Maple

Oh yeah, she wants me.

$\mathcal{A}$utumn

FROM: Congregation Simcha Aliz
SUBJECT: Last Minute Tickets!

Okay Members, if you have not already, now is the time to register for the High Holidays! Rosh Hashanah is just two weeks away and we have a ton of special options planned.

[...]

And don't forget! Stick around after Rosh Hashanah morning services, or come early for afternoon, to be a part of an immersive #SaveTheBees event planned by our very own recent grad, Anna Blue!

Anna wants to remind you all to look around for some yard space since there will be arboreal and floral take-home surprises! (We think it's just the bees-knees.)

[...]

P.S. learned from The Xerces Society: "Of the roughly 3,600 species of bees in North America, more than 90 percent lead solitary rather than social lives." Wow! You don't need to be a solitary bee, so come to Rosh Hashanah to learn more about how you can support them.

Nineteen — Tali

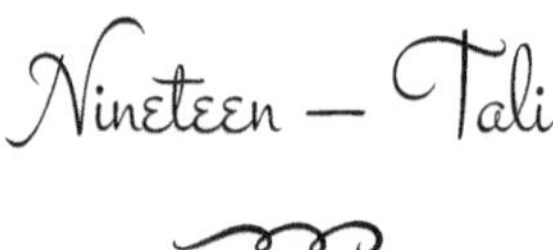

The following weeks were a mess of High Holiday preparation and family dinners with endless cousins and friends of the family. The Welcome Home Beth Dinner Tour.

Maple seemed to be in overdrive getting the project done for the temple and wrapping up some application she was being incredibly mysterious about.

Tali was glad for the distractions. She was still sorting through what their conversation about their fears meant and how to move forward.

It was an otherwise normal Friday night when all of it came to a screeching halt.

They were wrapping up the Shabbat service and moving into the lobby for snacks and chatting. Most of the attendees said their goodbyes and left, but a good group of fortyish people, including many of her teens, headed to the lobby.

Tali got there first to make sure everything was set. As usual, there was no reason to worry. Her colleagues had set it up perfectly. Except the cookie tray. Simon's latest attempt at appeasing his unnamed harasser had been tampered with. The cookies had been rearranged into the word "Anon" and a frown made of cookie bits was next to it.

She spotted it from a whole table away and was making her way to fix it before Simon could see when one of her coworkers got there first, restacking the dessert with gloved hands. *Great, nothing to worry about then.*

Her community filed in, grabbing drinks and snacks, grouping into little clusters around the room. As usual, the teens all broke away from their family units and clustered together arguing loudly about something Tali couldn't hear. She watched as Simon walked up to them and engaged them easily in a conversation about his interpretation of the week's Torah portion.

She was deciding how best to look busy, since there was clearly no way to be useful, when Anna rocketed into the room.

"Where were you?" Tali asked, an eyebrow raised.

"I went to the bathroom, weirdo." Anna rolled her eyes but couldn't contain herself long enough to commit to it. A smile split her face and she started hopping up and down. "But Tali! I got distracted!"

"Anna! By what!" Tali jokingly matched her sister's cadence, assuming the news would be about any one of her recent obsessions.

Anna turned her phone to face Tali. She took it from the teen and held it closer. *Okay, yeah, definitely time to get glasses. Sigh. Simon will never let you hear the last of it.*

After reading a line or two, she scrolled back up to see who the email was from and then back down to read the email again.

"Tali!" Anna said, laughing and practically vibrating. "Say something!"

"How did this happen already?" Tali asked, searching the

email again for the answer. "It's nowhere near Rosh Hashanah."

"I told you a million years ago, but you were so busy telling me no. The application was due last week, and it's like a really involved process, so they have you submit progress reports along the way. I've been updating them since we started working with Maple."

Her sister's face was radiant. She'd gotten in. She was going to Germany. She was going to Germany that coming spring.

The room felt like it might be spinning and she was suddenly very aware of how damp her armpits were. She needed to leave and get some air. But she also needed to be here, be Anna's sister.

"Anna," she said, making her voice as bright as she could. "This is incredible! You did all of that without telling me?"

"Yeah." Anna looked slightly sheepish at the admission. "I mean, you were super busy. But also, I wanted to prove I could do it. That I really deserved to get in, even with you helping me."

"You don't need to prove anything to me." Tali said. "I'm so proud of you."

"I know you are. And I know I don't." Anna fidgeted for a second, taking her phone back from where Tali still held it close to her face. "I needed to prove it to myself. It's a big deal and I've never been away from home. Away from you."

Tears knocked at the back of Tali's eyes, but she held out. "You'll always have me. I'll be a call away now instead of a room away."

"We'll have to figure out time zones," Anna said, turning to the practical. "I don't want to be like—"

"Beth," they said in unison and laughed.

"Anna, why don't you go tell your friends and I'll meet you by the car in a bit?"

Her sister gave her a curious look, but just nodded and bounced over to the group of teens. Many of them, like Anna, had graduated last spring, but were together in the limbo of youth between high school and whatever came next.

Tali beelined for the front door of the temple, doing her best to avoid being noticed by any of the congregation.

The air was humid, but the wind was a welcome relief on her sweaty neck. She found a bench and slid onto it, trying to get her breathing into a calmer pattern.

Anna was leaving. Beth was back but living in an apartment twenty minutes away and generally unwilling to be helped. Her grandparents had made it clear they loved having her there, but didn't need her. Even Simon had found a way to patch up his relationship without her, and was having his girlfriend, soon to be fiancé, read over his speeches instead of her.

She felt herself sinking into a vacuum. She'd lost her purpose. She tried to remember that she used to have one internal to her, that had driven her to apply to rabbinic school in the first place. Through the thrumming feeling of being left behind, she realized that was the thread she needed to pick back up.

And more than that, it's what she wanted. When she'd received her advisor's email encouraging her to return, she'd buried the feeling of desire beneath a mountain of self-imposed obligation. But now that she knew it, she couldn't let herself keep doing it.

She was going back to school.

A full minute of pure exhilaration at the idea passed before the sinking dread of reality set in. *What does that mean for me and Maple?*

"Okay, but when are you going to tell your girlfriend?" Her mother's voice crooned through the phone. Maple rolled her eyes. After their talk about feelings, she'd rode a wave of confidence right into telling her mother about Tali.

She regretted that decision now. Every conversation with her mother for the last several weeks ended up being a one-sided interview. Her mother wanted to know everything. Wanted to hear Maple gush about her feelings and give exact measurements for how short she was. What were her feelings on children? Was she allergic to anything? What were her parents like? Oh, a complicated family dynamic? That could be good for character! But was also something to watch out for when they had their own children. Did she want to come to Rosh Hashanah seder and meet the family?

"Ma!" Maple laughed even while she dragged a hand down her face. She realized too late it was her smudging hand and a quick glance at her reflection revealed, yes, she had given herself charcoal sideburns. "Enough, please. You'll meet her soon. You can ask her all sorts of questions. She loves questions."

Maple chuckled to herself at the image of Tali trying to appease her mother. Oh, she was looking forward to it. Whenever that may be. No rush.

Except, I want to rush. I want to marry her and spend the rest of our lives telling my mother together to leave us alone about babies.

"Okay, okay. But are you going to tell her about this job?"

Maple had heard back that morning about the art teacher position. Not only was it hers for the spring, they were interested in her potentially teaching Ladino 101 as well. She had wanted to call Tali as soon as she hung up with her future boss, but had hesitated.

"We're in a good place right now," Maple told her mother, and herself. "And I'm seeing her on Rosh Hashanah, in two days. I'd prefer to tell her in-person."

"Fine. Don't frighten her. Tell her you'll be back. And long distance isn't that bad!"

"Are you worried she's going to dump me or something?"

"Yes! And you sound so happy, my love." Her mother turned away from the phone to yell at her father, asking for his confirmation that Maple was happier than she'd been in a long time. She heard his grunt in response. *Maybe that's why I understand my assistant.* "Don't break up. Bring her to seder."

"Okay, okay. Plan for her to come."

Later that night she called Tali, who answered sighing.

"Uh oh, bad day?" Maple asked as she lay back in her bed.

"I don't know where to start." There was the sound of traffic in Tali's background and the rhythmic clicking of a turn signal.

"Are you driving home now?" Maple asked in surprise. It was late, especially for Tali's job.

"Yeah, you're on speaker," Tali reassured her. "We had so many issues with the lights and sound on our run-through today. Tomorrow's the final prep day when Simon practices and I wanted to make sure it was all good before then."

"Damn, well did it get sorted?"

"It did." But something in Tali's voice told her there was more.

"Uh huh. So what else is up?" Maple sat up, a tension clenching in her stomach.

"We can talk about it when we see each other. I don't want to do it on the phone."

Well, that sounds fucking awful. "Are you breaking up with me, Tali?"

The sounds of Tali parking, unbuckling, and exiting the car in silence unfurled between them. Eventually she said, "I want to talk about this in-person. It's more complicated than that."

"I cannot believe this." Maple shook her head to herself. Just a few hours ago she was telling her mother how she was trying to figure out the right way to tell this woman she loved her.

"I didn't say I was breaking up with you!" Tali sounded bone-tired, but Maple pushed aside her sympathy. "Look, I'm sorry the way I approached this. Today sucked. I have big news and it might mean we need to cool it for a bit."

"I can't even begin to understand what that means," Maple seethed. "But you're right, we should talk about this in-person. I'll see you in two days."

"Maple—"

"No, Tali. Look, I'm a little heated right now." She took a deep breath. "I want to hear your news and talk it out, and you're right. Big stuff can wait until we're together."

"Okay." Tali sounded so far away. "Okay, good night."
"Good night."

Twenty-One — Tali

Like every year for the past seven, Tali sat herself in the farthest back seat in the auditorium and settled in for the show. It was her own private Rosh Hashanah service the day before the real one. Simon alway wanted to practice, have her catch any last minute phrases needing tweaking, and make sure the cheap seats still got a good, clear show.

She watched as her boss took the stage and tried to ignore the heavy weight in her stomach. She'd been feeling a consistent, thrumming dread in her gut ever since her conversation with Maple. And the closer it got to seeing her again, the worse it hurt.

The High Holidays were all about coming to terms with who you are, forgiving yourself and each other, and promising to do better. But how could she when the thought of Maple made her feel weak? She couldn't deal with growing any closer to her, only to lose her as she finally went back to chasing her dreams.

No, this wouldn't be the new year where everything changed for her. She wasn't ready.

Simon cleared his throat, spreading his arms melodramatically and greeting the empty room. Tali tried to summon up her normal feelings of joy and excitement. Of the wonder of the Jewish calendar resetting and being renewed. It felt buried deep under her own grief in a way it hadn't in years.

Most of the speech was what she'd read weeks before when he sent her an early draft. He was good at finding ways of turning the ancient story of creation into something present and urgent.

Then he got to the new stuff.

"The earth was destroyed because humankind was too violent, too unkind to one another. Because we enslaved one another, tortured, and withheld from one another. Things we've done again, time and time again. But the earth won't be destroyed by a deity this time. It'll be destroyed by our own actions. We're shepherds of the planet, meant to honor the land and keep it safe for generations. Instead, we poison it, take it for granted, curse it when we ourselves have hurt it."

The words weren't anything Tali hadn't realized before. But the collision of time, of Simon's genuine concern, of all of the debates and learning she'd done with Maple over the last seven months, shook her right to her core.

She wanted to be doing the work of repairing the earth. She wanted to finish rabbinic school and be useful to this ailing planet in whatever way she could. And she wanted to do it with Maple. They pushed each other in all the right ways, believed in each other, and learned together.

She made it through the rest of Simon's speech, trying her best to listen for any missteps, but as soon as he was done she shot out of her chair. She made it to the stage before he was done going over his own notes.

"Simon, I need council."

"Right now? Did you listen—"

"Yes, and like every year you've over rehearsed. You're

going to be great, I only have two notes. They're the same notes I've been giving you—"

"Stand up straight and stop breathing into the mic?"

"Yes."

"Okay, okay. I'm working on it." He straightened up as if practicing her advice right then and there. "What's up?"

"How do you know if you're in love?" She thought she might throw up right there with the weight of the question.

"Well, Tali, are you in love?" He smiled at her with a moony expression, his own opinion written across his face.

"I'd know if I'd fallen in love. I'd know if my obsessive thoughts about the way her arms looked while she was painting had turned into something *more*. If these stupid butterflies had taken a turn. So what if every time I see a bee I think about sending her a picture? I'd know—oh, shit."

"Yeah." Simon nodded. "Sometimes we need to be honest with ourselves about what we want. If we just listen, the answer's often already there."

"Thanks, rabbi." And she said it with love.

"What do you need?" He looked at her with all the generosity in the world and it broke through the last wall Tali Blue had built around her heart.

"To be brave."

The next morning she woke up to Anna thrusting a cup of coffee into her hands.

"It's game day, Tal!" Anna was already dressed in her new year's best, her head newly-shaven. "Up, up, up."

She grumbled her thanks, downing as much of the hot

beverage as her mouth would allow, and threw herself into the shower. Years of repetition had taught her that she needed to set herself up for success, so she'd laid out her clothes and bag the night before. Making it easy to get dressed and into the car on time.

Thanks, nighttime Tali. She was working on being kinder to herself.

"Are we picking up Beth on our way?" She asked Anna as she slid into the passenger seat.

"Naw." Anna shook her head. "Bubbe and Zayde are picking her up when they come for my program and the afternoon services.

"Cool." Tali put the car into gear. "Let's hit it, my little innovator."

Anna laughed and shoved her shoulder and they were off, headed into a new year.

Maple was there already, putting the final touches on her art installations in the lobby. She was wearing what Tali felt forced to call dress overalls. They were black and looked velvety. She'd put them over a white-on-white floral button-up and her fancy Doc Martens. Her hair was down, curling over her shoulders. She was breathtaking.

"L'Shana tova," Tali wished Maple a happy new year shyly. "It's good to see you."

"Anyada buena! Dulse i alegre. It's good to see you, too," Maple said, returning her greeting in Ladino. Tali felt inexplicably overwhelmed by it. It was so lovely to hear, especially in this place where she'd spent most of her Jewish life.

"We should talk." Tali took a step toward her and then

paused. She looked around them and gasped. The lobby had been transformed into a pollinator wonderland.

Anna's ritual station was bordered by bee-friendly native tree saplings for folks to take home and plant. On the table between the baby trees were pledges to heal the earth. There were tables set up with information about places to volunteer and donate, petitions to sign, and interactive puzzles that taught about wild bee conservation.

On the floor, there was a pathway taped out to look like a tree, with many different interlocking branches and options for guests to follow.

Tucked into the corner was a framed lifesize photo of Tali, eyes closed, lips slightly parted, hands raised to the sky. Dripping in honey. She felt a tiny stir of revulsion at the memory, but she also realized how serene she looked. *It's like some part of me knew I'd figure it out.* It felt like a love letter.

And surrounding it all was Maple's art. All made from recycled goods, mostly reflective and etched with flora and fauna so people could literally see themselves in a greener future. She'd also constructed a beehive out of discarded wood pieces to hold Anna's homemade seed bombs in the shapes of bees.

Anna had spent weeks figuring out how to make them with pollinator-friendly plants so people could make bee gardens around the city.

"Wow. Look at this."

"I told you," Maple said, coming to stand next to her and admire their work. "Your sister is pretty cool.

"You're pretty cool," Tali said in a voice that meant *I love you.* "Maple, I'm sorry about the other night. And I'm sorry I have to keep saying sorry. I'm working on my shit and I'm going to be better."

"Tali," Maple said, reaching out to take her hand. "Slow down. What was your big news?"

"I'm going back to school." She winced, afraid of watching the realization hit Maple. Instead, there was only that brilliant smile, pure pride and celebration.

"That's incredible! When? And also *since* when?" Maple pulled her in for a tight hug, but before Tali could return it, she was being pushed back to arm's length. "Tell me everything."

"Uh, well." Tal reached out to grip Maple's arms. "Honestly, I've been so inspired by you and your passion for your work. I reached out a long time ago. But recently I also realized that leaving school was the right decision, but never going back isn't what I want."

"I'm so proud of you." Maple laughed and pulled her in for another hug. She squeezed her back this time. They stood that way for a minute until they heard the doors open and the guests begin to trickle in.

Tali looked up at Maple. "But—"

"You're worried about long distance." Maple said it as a fact. And without any hint of concern on her own face. *Is this just more cockiness?*

"Well, I *was*." Tali reached out again and took her hands. "But I was listening to Simon talk about ecodisasters and war crimes yesterday and I realized I don't want to let you go."

"So romantic," Maple teased, but pulled her closer. "I don't want to let you go either."

"Really?" Tali looked up at her, wanting her to lean down and kiss her. Even though the lobby was pretty busy now. Even though in twenty minutes she'd have to start working.

"Really, but I have a question for you."

Twenty-Two — Maple

"Come home with me to my mom's seder tonight?" Maple loved the way Tali looked when they were this close. She seemed small, but strong and butch at the same time. She felt like Tali fit right against Maple's side.

"Yes." Tali's brows lifted and she smiled ear to ear. "I thought it was going to be a scary question."

"It *is* a scary question. Just wait until you hear the list of things my mother wants to ask you."

"You can prep me on the drive up," Tali said determinedly. "Flashcards and all. Let's swing by my house so I can grab some clothes for tomorrow."

"Oh, are you inviting yourself over for the night?" Maple teased, slipping her fingers between Tali's.

"Someone promised me some naughty things." Tali pitched her voice low, looking around them to make sure they weren't overheard. "And I plan to—"

But she stopped talking mid-sentence, cocking her head like a puppy to one side while she stared at something. "Oh, no, Larry!" Tali clutched her face in apparent horror, but laughter leapt from her lips.

Maple looked around them at all of the old men, trying to decide which of them might be the distressing Larry. "Who?"

"One of my teens." Tali pointed at a tall, lanky kid waving a cookie at the rabbi and animatedly telling some sort of story. "I've been meaning to check in on him, he's been creeping around. But now I think he might be in bigger trouble."

Tali started to trot off in their direction before reaching back and grabbing Maple's arm and pulling her along. They made it to the cookie conversation in time to hear Larry say, "Uh, yeah, thanks for being such a good sport."

Maple watched as the rabbi's jaw worked itself sideways for a few seconds, his cheeks flushed, before he reached out and snatched the rest of the cookie the teen was about to throw in his mouth.

"Larry, we're going to have a serious talk about the line between pranking and harassing next week. But for now, this is my cookie and you're not welcome to any of the remaining cookies."

They all watched as the teen shrugged and slunk off to a group of kids standing around the snack table. He glanced over his shoulder at them and then slowly picked up another cookie and shoved the entire thing in his mouth.

The rabbi just sighed.

"Simon, Larry was your cookie bully?" Tali asked, still watching as the teen picked up several more cookies to shove into his hoodie pockets.

"Cookie *bully*?" Maple interjected.

"You must be the artist." Rabbi Simon turned to her with a sudden warm smile and stuck out a hand. She glanced over at Tali who shrugged sheepishly. *Oh. He knows.* She returned his smile with her own and a firm handshake.

"I am. You must be the boss."

"I am. Great work. Everyone loves the art and the

campaign. Honestly, more people have come up to talk to me about all this than they ever do about my sermons."

"Definitely didn't mean to steal your thunder!" Maple laughed, fighting an urge to put an arm around Tali. They hadn't finished their conversation and they needed to. Soon. Right now maybe. She thought she might explode otherwise.

"No, not at all." Simon laughed. "It's good! Anything that gets people sticking around for the second half of the day is good. And I'll get them back on my side on Yom Kippur. That's the big one here anyway."

"Okay, but Larry—" Tali tried again.

"Yes, he's been the one leaving the bad cookie reviews. Thinks he's a comedian, but also that he was doing us all a great service." Simon shook his head, clearly more than a little amused despite himself. "And, not that I'm going to admit this to him, it has felt good to learn to bake and be able to bring some joy to the community in this small way."

"You *baked?*" Tali's mouth dropped open.

"I did. Dana, my girlfriend, I mean, my fiancé, gave me a few pointers. Apparently, she's a much better baker than her grandmother."

"Your fiancé?!" Tali was close to screeching and Maple put a hand on her back to anchor her.

Simon flushed and ducked his head. "Yeah, I asked her last night." He shot a glance at Maple. "After, you know, our little talk about love."

"Wow, Simon! Mazel tov!" Tali reached forward and hugged him. Maple wondered what love talk they'd had that had led to Tali wanting to make long-distance work and Simon proposing. Maybe it was the season for new beginnings.

"But Larry. He's in trouble," Tali said, voice stern as Maple had ever heard it.

"Oh, for sure. I plan to talk to him about healthy forms of

communication after the High Holidays. I'd have you do it, but since you're leaving us, I figure you'll have other things to worry about for the next few weeks." He winked and shot a knowing glance in Maple's direction.

Tali's cheeks colored, but before she could respond Simon was stolen away by a group of older women with some feedback about his newsletter.

"Never a dull moment," Tali said instead.

"Seems that way. Now that our cookie drama commercial break is over. Can we get back to our talk?"

"Yes, of course, thanks for being such a good sport." Tali stepped closer, her attention fully on Maple now. "I mean, you're always a good sport. Literally the whole time I've known you. And I've been such a bummer. Thanks for giving me so many more chances."

"Tali, we all have our own shit going on." Maple could feel her own body wanting to lean in closer as well, each moment becoming less conscious of how many people could see them. Tali's eager, vulnerable face was all she saw. "I'm glad you're working on yours, so we can make this happen."

"It's going to be hard." Tali's brow creased as she spoke. Maple fought the urge to bend forward and kiss the line. "Long distance, but we'll figure it out. I'll get a social media account for you. I'll tell all the strangers on the internet how proud I am of my hot, smart, butch, Jewish girlfriend."

Tali's face went a little starry-eyed and Maple wanted to bathe in the sudden lovey-dovey version of Tali. "Oh." Maple snapped out of her trance a bit. "About that. You see, well…"

"You've changed your mind already?" Tali laughed, but an edge of fear had crept into her expression.

"No, don't be ridiculous. I just don't want to sound like a stalker."

"What? Are you suggesting moving with me right now? Cause I mean—"

"Tali! Stop talking before you say something that makes me regret the rest of this sentence."

"Fine, fine." Tali grumbled and it was so cute Maple thought she might die. Now that they were properly dating she'd have to find new ways to annoy Tali so she could watch her grump all over the place.

"First of all, I didn't know you'd decided to go back yet, and I applied for that teaching position at the school. And I got it. So, I, too, will be spending a semester at your school."

Tali gaped, but Maple pushed on, needing to use the momentum of truth-telling to get it all out at once. "Also, I'm in love with you."

Maple was frightened she'd broken Tali. *Well, perfect. Too fast! She literally just realized she had feelings for you and here you are, confessing—*

"I love you too," Tali said, cutting off whatever nonsense Maple's brain had been concocting. "I realized it this morning, but I think it's been true for a while. I blame all your flirty text messages and all your sweet gestures. I have no idea why you're in love with me though!"

"Tali, don't. Of course, you do. I'm in love with your honesty and that kind, gooey center you think you're hiding under all your prickly words."

"Well then, I guess I can look past the fact that you're following me to school."

"Technically I think I applied *before* you decided to go back. So, you're following me," Maple said smugly.

"Oh, whatever," Tali fake grumbled. "Can you kiss me now please?"

"Right here?" But Maple was already stepping forward and reaching out for the woman she loved.

"Everywhere," Tali said with a smile as their lips met and a choir of cheers went up from the herd of teens, Anna loudest of all.

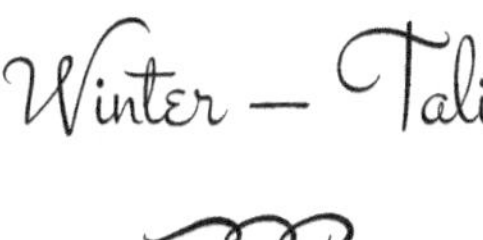

Winter — Tali

"That's the last box." Tali wedged it into the back of her car. Maple came around the side to wrap her in a hug as they looked at the Blue family home. "Okay, let's go before I cry again."

"It's a long drive," Maple reminded her. "And I'm still sad we're in two separate cars."

"Yes." Tali rolled her eyes. "You've said. So many times. I too will miss you uncontrollably for every minute we're apart."

"Have I ever told you how much sarcasm turns me on?" Maple pushed her up against the car and leaned in, sliding the tip of her tongue along the edge of Tali's lips.

"Lucky for you, that's all I've got." Tali leaned forward to deepen the kiss, gripping the back of Maple's head and yanking her hips against her own.

"I was thinking." Maple pulled back from the kiss. "Remember that weird secluded park we found like a month ago?"

Tali squinted at her. "Uh huh."

"Let's make a little pitstop there." Maple waggled her eyebrows as she skipped away to climb into her truck.

"Pervert," Tali called out to her, grinning and following in her own car.

When they got there, Tali parked behind Maple's truck and climbed out. Maple was already sitting in the bed of the truck, a blanket laid out.

"Join me." She patted the blanket and winked at Tali. Maple had installed steps on the back of her truck after the first time she realized Tali was too short to pull herself up onto it. She used those now to climb in and sit next to her girlfriend.

Maple was on her instantly, kissing her way along Tali's collarbone, pulling the straps of her tank top and binder out of her way. Tali let her head fall back and hummed at the nice sensation.

When the taller butch reached her mouth, their tongues slid against one another. Tali bit Maple's lower lip, tugging it forward until she gasped and then she returned the favor.

Maple swung a leg over Tali, pushing her onto her back. She unbuttoned Tali's pants, crawling backward and pulling them with her.

Tali thought about the empty field they were in, about being seen, but those thoughts were quickly chased away as Maple lowered her mouth to Tali's stomach. She kissed a path to the waistband of her boxers, stopping there to suck and nip at the skin.

Tali's hips came off the truck bed at the sensation and Maple laughed at her. "We haven't even started, short stuff."

"Well, get to it."

"So bossy." And then her mouth was on the boxer fabric covering Tali's pussy. Maple huffed out a hot breath before taking one of Tali's lips in her teeth and gently pulling. The feeling of soft fabric and sharp, sweet pain made Tali moan.

She reached up and pulled her binder up, rolling her own nipples between her fingers. She knew the moment Maple saw because she was rewarded with a deep guttural groan right against her clit.

"Are you going to eat my boxers while you eat me out?" Tali panted, tugging harder as the ache grew in her belly.

"Who told you that you could touch yourself?" Maple growled. She stuck her tongue out and licked the fabric along Tali's slit. "And I'll do what I want down here. You know I like to make you beg."

"Maple, please," Tali whined. "I can't handle it today. Please take them off."

"Since you asked so nicely." Maple yanked the boxers so roughly Tali thought they might tear. She didn't care. She shuffled her legs to get them as far down as she could so she could spread her legs. "But if you want me to let you come, you better pinch those things until I hear you whimper. Understood?"

"Yes." She did as she was told, rolling the hard buds of her nipples between her fingers and pinching their sensitive ends. "Anything."

"That's better," Maple said as she bent forward again. "I like you obedient."

And Tali thought she'd say something clever back, but her mind went blank at the first touch of Maple's tongue to her clit. She swirled it up and down the length, flicking off the tip each time. Tali used every ounce of willpower to not grab her head and grind against her. She still might if she thought she could get away with it.

Maple pressed a hand to Tali's stomach, as if sensing her desire to writhe. The other hand pressed against her thigh, slowly raking short nails down her skin. When Maple's lips closed around her clit and sucked, her body acted on its own, bucking hard up against her.

"Turn over," Maple said moving back.

"Wha—" Tali blinked, trying to clear her blurry desire out of her eyes. "Why?"

"Didn't you just take a shower?" Maple smirked at her and made an inpatient hand gesture to make her flip over. "On your hands and knees."

"I did, but—" She stopped, realizing what was coming and flushed. But she did as she was told. When she'd leaned down, resting on her forearms, Maple's strong hands gripped and spread her. She was sure she was blushing all the way to her toes, but her favorite kind of pleasure was in letting Maple use her body however she wanted.

Maple started back at her clit, sucking softer this time, following it with long, slow licks up through her folds. Moaning in appreciation of her taste. She pushed her tongue into Tali, one hand moving to stroke the exposed clit. When Tali's legs began to shake from being close to the edge, Maple stopped for a moment.

"Not yet, Tali," she reprimanded playfully.

"I can't hold out much longer."

"Yes, you can." There was a moment of stillness and then one of those perfect butch hands landed with an earsplitting smack on her ass. Tali moaned and shivered. "Again?"

"Please," she begged.

Maple rubbed her hand over the skin, warming it up. She delivered three quick smacks before gripping the cheek roughly.

"Fuck," Tali groaned, shaking her ass side to side to displace the pain and the pleasure.

"You want more?" Maple asked in what Tali had come to know as her top voice.

"I do, but not in this field." Tali laughed. "Someone will come."

"That could be fun," Maple teased, but she didn't move to

do it again. She moved her hand back to Tali's soaking wet pussy, ever so gently stroking her clit.

The first touch of Maple's tongue on her ass was almost enough to make Tali come. She fought down a scream.

"Oh, fuck." Tali moaned the words until they became a chant as Maple dragged her tongue in firm circles around her tight entrance, while keeping a steady tempo on her clit.

"Can I come?" She gritted out, pushing back against Maple's mouth.

"Nuh uh," Maple denied her.

She groaned and tried to keep the orgasm from pulling her under, tried to keep riding the wave of sensation building between Maple's mouth and finger without drowning.

And her tongue pushed ever so gently into her and Tali lost all control.

They came down together after Tali re-dressed in a sweet snuggle, Maple's head on Tali's chest. Both of them running gentle hands over the other and murmuring nonsense love words.

"There's one more thing I need to do before we hit the road."

They stopped at the synagogue, parking the moving van on a side street, and slipping into a backdoor so they wouldn't be interrupted by more goodbyes.

The last few weeks, maybe months, had been tons of goodbyes for both of them. Maple at least knew she was likely coming back after her teaching semester was over. She had rented out her studio and the apartment above it just for the length of her classes. So, her conversations had mostly been see-you-laters.

Tali had found herself feeling much mushier, weepier than she'd expected. She had no idea if she'd come back right away. She hoped Simon would hire her on as the junior rabbi, but six months was also a long time. She and Maple had talked about the possibility of needing to do long distance.

It'll be fine. We're good at texting.

They made their way through the temple hallways and Maple stopped at the doorway to Tali's office.

"No, come this way." Tali grabbed Maple's hand and urged her on. Finally they made it to Simon's office.

Tali let go of Maple's hand, and the taller butch seemed to realize she should stay in the doorway for whatever this was. Tali wasn't even sure what she was doing.

But her body knew what it needed. Her feet led her straight to her chair, the chair that had held her as she wept after her mother's funeral, that had contained her muted excitement when she accepted the job, that had served as a safe space to land over the last seven years.

She ran her hand over the back of it, feeling only a little foolish as she tried to tell it how grateful she was for everything.

Tali turned back to Maple, who was watching her with eyes too sweet and understanding.

"Let's get out of here."

And so they did.

Acknowledgements and Further Reading

Endless gratitude first and foremost to my partner who makes me believe all my wildest dreams are possible. And to my friends who are nice to me even when they don't understand what I'm ranting about.

To my beta readers, editors, and sensitivity readers who make everything better. Any mistakes are my own, and there'd be a lot more without these folks.

And a huge thank you to each person who takes a chance on me and buys one of my books.

I gathered SO much information I didn't end up putting into the book since this is a romance and not an ecology text. So, here are articles, books, and podcasts I've read all or part of, or listened to, about pollinators I recommend if you want to learn more:

- *Bees in America: How the Honey Bee Shaped a Nation*, by Tammy Horn
- *Farming on the Wild Side: The Evolution of a Regenerative Organic Farm and Nursery*, by Nancy J. Hayden and John P. Hayden
- *Fruitless Fall: The Collapse of the Honey Bee and the Coming Agricultural Crisis*, by Rowan Jacobsen
- Ologies Podcast, hosted by Alie Ward
- Especially: "Melittology (BEES) with Amanda Shaw," "Spheksology (WASPS) with Eric Eaton,"

and "Wildlife Ecology (FIELDWORK) with Corina Newsome"
- *Organic Manifesto: How Organic Farming Can Heal Our Plant, Feed the World, and Keep Us Safe*, by Maria Rodale
- *The Beekeeper's Lament: How One Man and Half a Billion Honey Bees Help Feed America*, by Hannah Nordhaus
- *The Forgotten Pollinators*, by Stephen L. Buchmann and Gary Paul Nabhan

Other notes and resources:

- If you're curious to learn and read more about stone identity, I recommend this incredible essay by Xan West, z"l: https://xanwest.wordpress.com/2014/03/09/what-is-stone/
- Also, if you've never read *Stone Butch Blues* by Leslie Feinberg, z"l, add that to the list.
- For US readers who want more information on what plants are native to your area (and make for happy pollinators) check out: https://www.nwf.org/nativeplantfinder/
- If you want to learn to build a bee condo so your wild solitary bees have a nice place to live near your native garden, here's that link: https://www.chicagobotanic.org/plantinfo/building_bee_nesting_block
- Interested in learning Ladino? www.myjewishlearning.com/article/how-to-learn-ladino/

Also, I am ALWAYS interested in learning more, so if you have recommendations, email them to rozalexanderwrites@gmail.com or tweet them at me: @writesroz

Finally, as a sendoff gift, if you want to see the cutest pollinator out there, look up the Honey Opossum.

Matzo Match Sample

"*Matzo Match by Roz Alexander is the erotic, Passover romance novella that you never knew you needed….It's sweet, sexy, and kind of angsty. Make sure to pick it up, no matter what time of year it is.*" —*The Lesbian Review*

Looking for more queer, Jewish romance? Read on for the first chapter of Matzo Match. (And meet Maddy's sister, Virginia!)

Purchase it here: books2read. com/matzomatch

Sam shot out of bed seconds after her alarm began playing its latest Pop Top 100 selection, pulled on the first clothes she found, and left her apartment an hour before she'd normally leave for work to run as fast as she could to the grocery store. The whole way, she imagined she'd make it there before any other customers if the empty streets indicated anything.

Still, she found herself chanting, "Please still have matzo, please still have matzo, please still have matzo," under her breath. It was only a few days away from night one of Passover, and she was way, way, way behind. So behind that when her mother had called her the night before to just chat and casually asked how the preparation was going Sam had stifled a whimper of shame.

Luckily, Virginia was coming over that evening after work to help her clean, including getting rid of all of the leavened bread products in her house. Sam thought she could probably convince her to do some light crafting too. Decor was at least 90% of why Sam loved to host, and she wouldn't skimp on it this year just because she was way off her timeline. It thrilled her to set a table with carefully coordinated table mats, dishes on top of larger dishes, delicate wine glasses—all set around floral arrangements and origami and paper cuttings. Candles! She needed some more candles too.

Most of all, she needed matzo. She could not believe she'd let it get so close to Passover without securing at least ten boxes of the holiday's tasteless, flatbread. Fool! Not only did she need two boxes for her matzo toffee crackle she'd serve after her own seder, she needed two more boxes for the crackle she planned to bring to Cara and T's. Plus, it was all she'd eat for the next week—matzo with eggs for breakfast, matzo pizza for lunch, matzo ball soup for dinner—until she was so sick of it, she'd be happy to not see it again for a year.

She arrived before the store even opened, so she took the time to stretch her legs and hips, her muscles happily humming from the run. Thank you, weather, she thought, so tired of having to run indoors on a treadmill. Breathing deeply and lifting her arms high overhead, she worked on calming her pounding heart. Once she felt a stillness settle over her, she took a seat on the nearby bus bench. Folding her arms over her chest, she realized she'd left everything but her credit card and keys at home. Somehow, she'd also managed to put on two different sneakers in her haste to get out the door.

Great, just perfect, she inwardly groaned, but desperate to hold onto the post-sprint peace, she forced herself to take in the beautiful, crisp day.

It was an early day of spring and looking up at the tiny green buds on the tree overhanging the bus stop nearly brought tears of joy to her eyes despite all of that morning's stress. This had always been a big part of why she loved Passover so much. Even when she was a kid—and her siblings would whine and bargain to get out of sitting through the full Passover experience—Sam had loved that it felt like a way of welcoming in the freedom and history of her people and of the world around them. She made a mental note to make sure she bought a lot of flowers to decorate around the seder plates this year.

Look at me, Ms. Positivity over here, Sam wondered to herself. And, she continued, honestly, if I can manage to get these thoughts back on track, maybe it is time to start thinking about Pauline. Sam knew Virginia wasn't wrong, that she'd have to move on sometime. And it's spring! Love was basically perfuming the air.

Sam had been staring so intensely up at the tree in deep thought that she hadn't realized someone was now standing quite close to her. Her heart gave a little jump as she spotted them out of the corner of her eye, and she realized it was one of the sexiest people she'd ever seen.

The stranger had short hair, cropped down to stubble on the sides and back, and started to go salt-and-pepper on the side closest to Sam. Their crisp white button-up was tucked into dark jeans over camel-colored work boots. They were tall and leaning in profile to Sam against the bus sign pole, looking so at ease that Sam worried they'd actually been there before.

Had they witnessed Sam's frantic dash to the storefront, her ridiculous attempt to yank open a clearly locked door, and, most embarrassing of all, her luxuriating in post-run pleasure?

No, she felt confident she would have noticed someone so blazing hot even in her matzo-less distress. Especially someone who wore jeans like they were painted onto their body, the outline of a slim wallet clearly visible in the butch's back pocket.

Sam realized she was staring at this stranger's tight, denim-clad ass at the same moment she realized the stranger was looking at her with amusement. The stranger's eyes were a rich brown, just a few shades darker than their skin. Their full lips curved wickedly up at the corners and startled a tiny but audible gasp out of Sam.

The sound seemed to stoke their amusement, their smile widening to reveal blindingly white teeth.

Sam felt flames lick up from her chest to turn her pale neck and cheeks scarlet. Her rib cage now a furnace of mortification, Sam was convinced she was visibly sweating far more than she had on her run. She immediately jumped up, gripping her keys hard in one hand, and fled to the now-open grocery store's front doors.

Find it here: books2read.com/matzomatch

Other Books in the "Hot for the Holidays" Series

Read them in any order (though I suggest their numbered order). They share a universe and you'll see your favorite characters in the background of the other stories.

Matzo Match: An Age Gap Lesbian Romance

"Matzo Match by Roz Alexander is the erotic, Passover romance novella that you never knew you needed....It's sweet, sexy, and kind of angsty. Make sure to pick it up, no matter what time of year it is." —*TheLesbianReview*

"I read it in five hours and it would have been four except I had to stop in the middle to take a cold shower. If you're into high heat queer romance, this one's for you." —BookishlyJewish.com

"[Jordan] may be the most delicious butch I've read to date. Just as I felt when I read my beloved novellas from Erin McLellan's So Over the Holidays series, I wanted to be in this story at the Seder with the queer friend group. Overall, this novella was very sexy and it also made me laugh out loud - my favorite combo!" —AnaCoqui.com

Can a meddling matchmaker help two broken hearts to love again?

After a brutal break-up, Sam is ready for a lot of things: spring, hosting on her own again, a casual fling or two. Sam is definitely not ready for anything real, but her best friend Virginia has decided she's taken long enough. When loving encouragements aren't enough, Virginia takes fate into her own hands.

With Passover just around the corner, will a surprise blind date, three celebrations in eight days, and approximately 100 glasses of wine be enough to finally move on?

After one taste of the hard-bodied, immaculately dressed butch Jordan, it just might be time. Too bad Jordan has her own baggage to work through.

Matzo Match is a steamy lesbian age gap love story and the first entry in the "Hot for the Holidays" series.

A Masc for Purim: A Sapphic Second-Chance Romance

Does true love have an expiration date? What about forgiveness?

Every year, tomboy-femme Liza plans the perfect party for Purim, and every year she goes alone. She's convinced her role as holiday host is enough to find happiness, but lately, the nights have gotten lonelier.

Carrie, a.k.a. Liza's first love, a.k.a. the butch who broke her heart into a million pieces, is back in town and determined to win Liza back. Carrie has spent the last ten years unlearning the internalized ableism that reared its head after her diagnosis of progressive vision loss.

And ten years of regretting leaving Liza.

Their inexperience and inability to be vulnerable with one another may have driven them apart the first time, but has the last decade taught them both to be brave? Luckily, they have the whole megillah to figure it out.

A Masc for Purim is an angsty, steamy, second-chance romance novella between a bisexual butch and her tomboy lesbian.

A Year of Firsts: A Sapphic Toaster Oven Romance

Two people on a journey of self-discovery + a to-do list of 18 experiences = a surprising love story.

CJ has always known what they want out of life: to be a loud, proud queer, to be a part of a community, and to adopt as many puppies as they're legally allowed to own. So far, they're one for three.

In order to answer some of the biggest questions hanging over them, they're paired together with quiet classmate Mia to create a list of 18 experiences to have over the next year.

Mia started considering Judaism for her husband, but a year after their painful divorce she realizes she still wants to explore Jewish community for herself. Her only problem is keeping all the information in her head during her dyspraxia flare-ups.

One year to figure out who they each want to be…and who they want to love. CJ and Mia realize some questions come with surprising answers.

A Year of Firsts is a sapphic (nonbinary + queer woman), "toaster oven," romance about learning to trust yourself.

About the Author

A child of multiple diasporas, Roz (they/them) has always been obsessed with the idea of home being how you love another person. Their books focus on that idea while showcasing characters of many intersections of identities—plus a little humor, a heavy pour of steam, and a dash of angst.

They are a physically/progressively disabled, white, trans person with ADHD and have more interests than time in the day. You can find them spoiling their three terrible cat-beasts; connecting to their Jewish culture through moon-worship, plantcraft, and cooking traditions; and making weird art when they're not writing or stewarding a native pollinator garden with their beshert.

Stay in touch, sign up for their newsletter: https://signup.rozalexander.com